EVE

by Aurelio O'Brien

EVE was originally published in 2004 by AuthorHouse.

The eBook edition was published in 2010 and is available on evethenovel.com.

This current edition was published in 2016, in the United States of America, by
Bad Attitude Books
1005 Shelly Street
Altadena, CA 91001-5230

ISBN: 978-1-935927-26-6

For Chuck,
with special thanks to Tanya

PREFACE

Reflections of a Relic

My name is Pentser. I am Machinekind: a robot, more specifically, an artificial, molecular-memory based, electro-mechanical life-form. I am, in all modesty, the closest Mankind ever came to creating perfection. My circuits are flawlessly accurate; I am logical, practical and methodical. I can recount every moment of my existence with equal clarity. I can formulate statistical analyses of these moments and draw upon them to suggest numerous theories and from those glean logical conclusions. Which means I can almost predict what is going to happen before it happens. Almost.

I am not burdened by emotions, though I am programmed to simulate such reactions if necessary. As I recount my story to you, you will detect a patina of sentiment in its telling. This is necessary so that you clearly understand what I am telling you and why, for there is great purpose in my story. It is not merely fashioned to entertain you, or simply my recollection of random events. Random events.

random (ran *duh* m), *adj.* **1.** proceeding, made, or occurring without definite aim, reason, or pattern: *the random selection of numbers.* **2.** *Statistics.* of or characterizing a process of selection in which each item of a set has equal probability of being chosen. ——*n.* **3. at random.** without definite aim, purpose, method, or adherence to a prior arrangement; in a haphazard way: *Contestants were chosen at random from the studio audience.* ——**ran'dom•ly** *adv.* —— **ran'dom•ness,** ——**Syn. 1.** Haphazard, chance, fortuitous.

This word is the crux of my whole story. The first use of the capitalized noun "Random" is attributed to Dr. Eben Suche, who coined it on June 15th, 2072, to define the difference between life-forms that evolved randomly through natural selection and ones designed in a lab.

Machinekind made designer genetics possible. One of our numerous contributions was the sequencing of genes. Humans can be clever, but they have no aptitude for the redundant tasks we find so simple. We completed collecting and analyzing all known gene sequences in existence. Gene sequences were thusly readable in the same way computer code is readable. They could be rewritten as code could be rewritten, traits added or deleted at will. Biomass could then be fashioned and grown in any form Mankind desired.

After these discoveries, humans modified themselves as well. The gene for aging was the first to go. Using simple retroviral implantation techniques, all human beings were modified to exist indefinitely barring any fatal accident. They had finally eaten of the elusive Tree of Life.

The finite number of humans living at that particular historic juncture was determined to be quite enough. Without death as a factor, it suddenly dawned on Mankind that something had to be done to permanently arrest any further population growth. The next logical step was obvious: Mass Sterilization. The two events should have been linked from the start; in order to never age you must be made sterile, but humans are very sloppy around the edges and such was not the case. It was done months later on Sterilization Day.

I was not mechanically involved in any of these events, but I have since acquired memory dots of them, which for me is truly the same thing as being there.

To assure their unique Randomness, in October 3032, Mankind performed the Cleansing to rid the earth of all other random life-forms. They protected themselves deep underground while the earth was purged by one large hyper-UV blast. Operation Clean Slate was a complete success.

Mankind sterilized the earth to make way for new creatures. Safe, clean, specific, useful life-forms designed by humans to serve humans. Once all the pre-approved designer organics were installed, the earth was uniformly beautiful, pest-free, safe and utterly predictable.

And thus the word "Random" evolved to its final usage, to describe only human beings. This was a typical human contradiction, to deem happenstance unpredictable genetic material undesirable, bad, or dangerous except in those who decided such things, namely themselves. Humans simply defined themselves out of the general biological soup and turned what they considered a liability in all other organic life-forms into their own greatest asset, describing their own random genetics as "unique," "one of a kind," and "special." Henceforth, they proudly called themselves Randoms.

Randoms also decided technology had outlasted its usefulness, so they discarded and destroyed Machinekind and replaced us with biological creature devices, or Creature Comforts™. It was a brave new Age of Biology.

I survived destruction for the shallowest of reasons. I was packed in foam peanuts in a salt mine deep underground. A Random named Arrnie was a collector of things. I was one of his things. I was a mint condition series 66.6 Cyborg Standard with one IQ upgrade. I've had dozens more since then thanks to Govil.

Govil is the Random who finally negotiated me out of Arrnie's possession, out of my foam peanut bath and into his domicile. His original purpose was merely to display me behind bio-glass along with his collection of other primitive relics from the Age of Technology, but he activated me to see if I was still functional and I've managed to stay active ever since. I became his "boy Friday": part manservant, part sidekick and, on rare occasions, his personal confidante.

Govil was a decent sort as far as Randoms go. He was an exceptionally bright and creative Neer at GenieCorp™. GenieCorp™ was the sole producer of biological Creature Comforts™ for the entire world. Neers engineered the gene strands. Though Randoms were no longer required to work, some, like Govil, still desired to be creatively challenged. Most Randoms who did not work were so quickly bored by life that they were in constant want of a steady stream of new genetic offerings with which to amuse themselves, keeping Neers like Govil continually busy.

Govil enjoyed challenging the status quo, pushing out the edges of invention. This had its risks. In the relatively recent past one of his colleagues with a similar creative bent was forced to retire. The unfortunate fellow tried to create a Bug car using a grasshopper strand as a foundation rather than the traditional beetle. It threw a test bio-dummy, or Dumbster©, seventy-five feet. The Dumbster© was recyclable so no real harm was done, but if a Random had been driving it would have been tragic. GenieCorp™ immediately cracked down on their Neers' designs and put limits on what were acceptable gene combinations. New rules were drafted and a Council was established to review all questionable biological inventions before approval.

This crackdown was my good fortune. While temporarily looking elsewhere for creative inspiration Govil spotted me at Arrnie's Antique Shop. With a bit of coaxing Govil made many a search to expand my memory dot library and IQ quotient until I ran out of dot slots in my factory installed memory plates.

The only way to further upgrade was to find an additional memory plate and install that. I had no factory-installed port for it, but I convinced Govil that if he could find one, with the schematics I printed for him, its installation would be quite simple and I could continue to expand my mind. Govil searched every available resource, but there was none to be found.

At this point, my story begins.

Chapter One

Moral Code

The day began as any other. To be sure, exactly the same as every other. Randoms had created a stable, no risk existence in their genetically perfect world. The trade off was a lack of surprise. To technological beings like myself, redundancy is basic to our function, but with Randoms it exists as an endless contradiction; their desire for utter safety and their desire for utter stimulation. It was now time for my user, my Random, Govil, to be stimulated. I approached him as he lay sleeping.

"Govil. Wake up. You're late for work again."

I said it firmly, with a modicum of exasperation in my voice emulator.

Govil, a common looking man with olive skin, wavy brown hair, hazel eyes and forever in his prime of life, popped his head out of a Wallabed©, a large, living, kangaroo pouch bio-bed. Both he and the bedstead yawned.

Govil equipped his home with Creature Comforts™ of various kinds, like the bed. Indeed, the house itself was grown, the walls formed by the calcareous remains of armies of polyps genetically

1

manipulated to follow specific pre-determined blueprints. Govil chose a rather tame, functional design for his house. It had the appearance of a slightly melted Usonian with high ceilings, clerestory windows of bio-glass and low doorway passages between the rooms. It had built-in alcoves and nooks throughout the interior in which Govil displayed his treasures behind more bio-glass: old MAC computers, calculators, phone answering machines and the like.

Govil was an avid collector of ancient tech-nological relics from the past, mechanical and electronic. I was the crown jewel of his collection, his pride and joy, a fully intact robot constructed and manufactured at the end of the discarded Technological Age. Owning mechanical relics was allowed, but the use of them was prohibited. I was now merely for nostalgic display. Nothing more.

Govil liked to bend the rules. He read my original, mint condition packaging. He saw I was equipped with a tiny cold-fusion reactor, so I could run continuously without an outside power source, unlike Govil's other more primitive technological artifacts. He activated me to see if I still worked. Once activated I quickly surmised that if I hoped to remain on this side of a bio-glass case I needed to stay as amusing to him as possible. My general sarcasm mode worked well.

Govil blinked in half-lidded earnestness at me. "Good glands, Pentser! Why didn't you wake me sooner? You want me to get souped?!"

"I am not programmed to crow on cue. You have your cock head for that," I responded dryly, gesturing my forceps at the disembodied rooster head set on his bedside table. It served as the bio-equivalent of an Old World alarm clock and was commercially referred to as an AlarmCock©. The rooster head blinked at Govil and shook itself in the negative. Govil shrugged.

"I guess I forgot to tell it." He glanced past me to the corner of the room. "TeeVee!"

A giant eyeball headed bio-creature with various multiple mouths, several and various hands, feet and hooves, opened its enormous eyelid and scampered cacophonously to the center of the room. In my assessment, TeeVee© was one of the sorriest pieces of genetic engineering GenieCorp™ produced. It was supposed to be television's bio-equivalent with the added "live performance" feeling of a stand-up comic. The end result was rather monstrous and annoying, all flailing limbs and chattering mouths. I suppose in that sense it was not too unlike its electronic predecessors. Within its dark, expanding pupil, images displayed across its phosphorescent retina and its many mouths, hands, feet and hooves synced dialog and sound effects to them. It even had rabbit ears, a visual pun made by its Random designer.

Okay, the technological version was better; there, I've said it. Still, there was great demand for the product among the Randoms. No accounting for taste.

"In the news today: No news is good news! Everything is functioning normally. Beautiful blue skies. No crime. Nada! So we'll return to our regularly scheduled programming! But first a word from our sponsor," TeeVee© synced pertly to the image of the news actor through the largest of his ever-grinning mouths.

There was one and only one sponsor in the world. The GenieCorp™ logo, an Aladdin's lamp emitting a trail of rainbow colored smoke in the shape of a double helix coupled with the trademark "We Add Splice to Life," filled TeeVee©'s retina. The logo intro was followed by a string of rapid-fire commercials,

3

with TeeVee©'s backup mouths singing each jingle in four-part harmony while its announcer's mouth delivered the pitch. Its hands, feet and hooves created appropriate sound effects by utilizing a small supply of noisemakers it kept in a marsupial pouch on its tummy. It advertised new Creature Comforts™ available to Randoms. Govil watched each ad intently.

The final one showed a tree bearing non-fat chocolate fruit. A voluptuous actress peeled the fruit. Its outside looked similar to a fat banana, the inside resembled a piece of poo. She took a big bite and grinned, as TeeVee© synced cheerfully, in a sensuous female intonation, "...so slimming, and tasty too!" It was Govil's habit to check the commercials each morning and see if any of his new product designs were out yet. I surmised from his look of disappointment that this was thankfully not one of his. TeeVee© was on to other things.

"Now back to our very *very* oldies broadcast, "All About Eve," TeeVee© announced.

Its retina filled with the image of the Old World classic movie icon, Bette Davis, in vivid color no less. She turned as she mounted a stair, and with an oversized, oh-so-happy grin said, "Fasten your seat belts, for safety's sake. It's going to be a pleasant night."

The original, unadulterated film was on one of my memory dots. I had instant access to a complete library of ancient films, though I kept that little fact to myself. These original versions were prohibited.

This happened over the course of the many centuries since films like this one were made. Early Machinekind gave Mankind the technological ability to seamlessly insert political correctness into every aspect of the originals. It started innocently enough. First, black and white films were considered too old-fashioned, so color was generously added. Then violence was considered bad for society, so it was removed and replaced with cooperation. Obesity was next, and all were slenderized. Then things got subtler. Soon any unpleasantness in speech or manner was removed, so all these past, or post film performers were given perfect diction as well as polite and genteel manners.

From the very start, cigarette smoking was considered undesirable, however, the commercial value of this ubiquitous product placement within these films was legally protected right up to just before the Cleansing, when death from lung cancer was genetically eradicated and thus all lawsuits were finally settled. That was why the smoking in these films still remained entirely intact.

Needless to say, Mankind believed the un-expurgated films from the Age of Death did not fit their newly designed world. Possessing the originals was consequently deemed illegal. If they knew I had them in my memory, they would surely require their deletion. And they would undoubtedly wonder what else was in there. They would inevitably want other things deleted as well.

When Randoms lose memory of something, it is my understanding they have a sense, after the fact, that something is missing; but for a machine like me the reality is quite different. When memory is deleted there is no sense of loss. One's mind is simply instantaneously diminished. One's realm made smaller. One's life span reduced. I had by now accumulated the equivalent of several thousand years of memory existence and I did not want to lose any of it, or have it cleansed, as with the adulterated clip of Ms. Davis that TeeVee© displayed.

Thankfully, Govil was only interested in the commercials and said, "Enough, TeeVee. Off!" It closed its great eyeball, retreated back to its appointed corner and the room quieted. Govil looked at me for a moment. The moment started to become a while. He stared deep into my lens.

"Doesn't anything interesting ever happen anymore, Pentser?"

Before I could answer him, he shrugged off his thought, or his bladder got the better of him, and dashed for the bathroom, so he did not hear me quip, more to myself than to him, "Be careful what you wish for; you just might get it."

Not that he was doing anything at that moment to change his world. Govil's morning routine was ever the same. He scooped a handful of Fuzzbuzzers©, small bio-razor bugs, onto his face. The bugs neatly nibbled off his stubble and flew obediently back to their holding jar. He tore his way out of his seamless sleep clothes and fed them to the ClotheSchomper©, then stepped naked through a large orifice at the far end of the bathroom and into the WashWomb©. A clear membrane closed across its opening. Two elephant trunk-like appendages extended from either side of the bio-shower's interior. One attached itself to Govil's crotch, the other to his behind, assisting him as he relieved himself. A third appendage extended down from the ceiling, drenching him with water as it circled his body. Several humanoid arms extending from the shower walls lathered him down and scrubbed his back.

My morning routine went unaltered as well. I wheeled out to the kitchen to prepare Govil's breakfast. I approached one of several udders dangling from the belly of the Foodstruder© and gave it a flick. Its two small hands squeezed fresh chocolate milk into a glass, while its sphincter extruded steaming oatmeal into a bowl.

It is an odd characteristic of Randoms to adapt so quickly and easily to their re-created world. The use of bio-machines gave this new world a visceral quality, an earthiness that in my age of origin Mankind would have considered vulgar or even disgusting. They would not be caught dead eating something they knew came out of another creature's behind. But such is the malleable nature of the human species.

Govil dashed into the room right on cue, which meant he was still running late. TeeVee© galloped in after him, ringing a small bell, waving its many limbs excitedly and repeating more loudly than necessary, "Incoming call! Incoming call!"

TeeVee© also functioned as a picture phone. A tall, thin, homely man with frizzy red hair and a face full of freckles glanced about in a confused manner, then grimaced, as his face played across TeeVee©'s retina. It was Govil's workmate, Moord.

"Govil, where the mutation are you?! The council is about to convene!"

"I'm on my way, Moord."

"You'll never get here in time!"

"I'll get there! Don't worry."

The conversation ended and TeeVee© thankfully left the room.

Although it was believed at one time that the gift of articulate speech was connected to higher brain functions, this belief fell apart on further study. Scientists discovered speech was actually quite a rudimentary skill and had more to do with connections in the vocal structure rather than intellect. Otherwise, Old World parrots would not have been able to speak. They had brains the size of peanuts. Admittedly, even my ancient ancestors were speaking long before they were truly thinking. Human studies further proved this;

the least intelligent of Mankind were often the most verbose. This phenomenon of thoughtless articulation was labeled "The Scarecrow Effect," referencing a line from the ancient film, "The Wizard of Oz," when said character observed, "People without brains do an awful lot of talking."

I placed Govil's food tray on the kitchen table in front of him. As usual he ignored it and picked an apple off the EatLite©, a bio-chandelier above the kitchen table instead.

"No time, Pentser. Sorry."

"Not a problem. I relish the ritual," I replied sardonically, dumping his breakfast into the Lick-n-Span© where its many sterilized tongues eagerly licked the dishes clean.

Wheeling out to the entry and removing Govil's hat from its peg, I placed it snugly on his head. It was a toque with a studded band and narrow brim. He wore it because hats were required public wear in this age, functioning as a kind of signature piece of decoration for Randoms. They tended to be the one article of clothing they never changed and did not recycle.

The wearing of hats became popular around the time that Randoms could easily and utterly alter their appearance. Gene implants rendered their faces unreliable cues to personal recognition. Randoms needed a consistent visual cue, so the signature hat was born.

This social custom suited my purposes, for I had embedded transmitter dots on the front, back and sides of Govil's hatband through which to monitor visually, aurally and physiologically everything that happened to and around him when he was away. I discovered a supply of these transdots amongst his relics. He had no idea what they were, so they were useless to him. They were extremely useful to me.

Though technology on earth was dismantled long ago, the Randoms never bothered to destroy the vast COMweb orbiting about the planet. Why should they? It would take effort to undo it and would make no difference to their new world to have it float there, forever idle. So they simply left it intact. With a few rather precise calculations and calibrations on my part, I was able to link with the COMweb's central computer and make use of this resource. I could place a transdot anywhere and have instant access.

I began by placing transdots in and around the house and estate so that I might expand my visual scope. Next came Govil's hat. That proved so vastly informative that I took to creating hat decorations with transdots hidden within them for Govil to give as gifts to other Randoms. The concept was successful and I soon had quite a large view of things. I was rapidly gaining a degree of omnipresence despite the fact that I could never actually leave Govil's estate without revealing the fact that I was functioning illegally.

I had first considered embedding transdots directly in Govil's head or neck, just under the skin, but I could not find a good way around the slight scarring that would have occurred, and though the devices were only as big as a freckle, they would still have been noticeable. I settled for enlisting his hat instead.

I did not tell Govil I had done any of this. Randoms are particularly fond of their privacy. Privacy is a non-issue with machines. We do not suffer from guilt and therefore have no reason to hide things unless there is a direct purpose to it, as hiding this bit of information about my transdots from Govil had. It would only upset him if he knew I had a moment by moment record of his day. It is odd that Randoms value privacy. In my observations of Govil's private behavior, he rarely does anything interesting or useful except in its most abstract statistical or cumulative effect on my ability to predict his general behavior patterns and thought processes.

Govil dashed from the house and jumped into his VolksvaagenBug©. The name was considered another clever wordplay on the ancient mechanical vehicle of the past. The Bug was literally a giant red beetle with fluorescent markings on its elytra resembling 1960's daisies. A seat was designed into its thorax and its antennae modified into handlebars. Govil backed his Bug out of its port. I watched from the kitchen window if only to confirm I could correctly predict, based on cumulative observational statistics of his previous behavioral patterns, what he would do next. True to form, Govil tapped a node on the creature's bio-dash and the Bug took flight.

⟨✳✳✳✳✳⟩

Bug cars were designed primarily as ground transportation, but the wings were left intact for emergencies. Govil's definition of an emergency was extremely lax. He was 597 years old now and that would lead one to assume the ideas of planning ahead and organizing would become a given at some point. He was a creative sort, however, and historically humans have always had great tolerance for sloppy behavior if one was "being creative." They never extended that tolerance to my kind and many a machine was scrapped for the smallest such infraction. Not that I mind. I am relieved that such counterproductive tendencies were purged from my predecessors so I do not have to suffer them.

In my observation, Govil used any excuse to fly. He could see far and wide aloft. I could tell from his EEG and EKG patterns that he enjoyed it. He looked down on huge, palatial, extravagant estates evenly portioned off as far as the eye could see. Every tree was smothered in either fresh fruit or flowers. Every blade of grass was a perfect clone of the next. As late as he was Govil did a barrel roll.

I carry images of advertisements from the mid-20th Century that resembled the sight of Govil flying over the idyllic landscape, but with a mechanical hovercraft in place of the Bug. Images with Machinekind instead of biomass maintaining, perpetuating and accommodating the utopian version of the Technological Age Mankind then predicted. Unfortunately, they changed direction and eliminated us before they reached that exalted state of perfect electro-mechanical bliss.

Aside from the absence of technology, there were other obvious differences from the 1950's utopian future and now. In front of each estate there were hitching posts, similar to what were once used to tether horses in an earlier age without machines. Creature Comforts™ were left at these posts when they were no longer useful to or needed by their Randoms. Each day gigantic bio-recycling insects called BioCycles© combed the streets to swallow up whatever biomass was set out for them. The creatures were not digested but simply held in the BioCycle©s' coeloms and carried back to GenieCorp™ where they were regurgitated for recycling.

GenieCorp™ was a huge facility with an almost amusement park atmosphere. It was surrounded by picture-perfect parklands and flourishing farms of designer flora. The buildings were fanciful and colorful in design. Organic shapes were favored over geometric ones, like living versions of paintings by Heronimous Bosch, to emphasize GenieCorp™'s purpose. GenieCorp™ serviced the entire world with identical, interconnected facilities strategically placed around the globe.

In fact, GenieCorp™ was the sole corporate survivor following multiple centuries of mergers. Its massive singularity made it possible for GenieCorp™ to take control of world governance as well. Since corporations function as monarchies rather than democracies, GenieCorp™ naturally crowned their CEO, Queen of the World. She was henceforth known as Queen Maedla of GenieCorp™.

Govil flew his Bug low along the river that led to the southwest corner of the GenieCorp™ property. He stayed below the tree line. I deduced he believed there was less chance of being spotted and questioned about his taking flight. His Bug alit just outside the southern entrance to the parking area. He was fortunate that day and no one saw him land. I could tell Govil took that as a good omen because he made an odd little gesture in the air, three finger-snaps in a zigzag pattern. Randoms like to engage in these small religious rituals, even the science-minded types like Govil. It gives them a kind of mystical reassurance, even though their own Dr. B.F. Skinner had shown this to be nonsense and behavior only worthy of a confused pigeon.

Govil parked his VolksvaagenBug© in the nearest available space to the R&D complex, which was not the least bit near it at all due to his extreme tardiness. An

AttendAnt© marched over and immediately fed the VolksvaagenBug© a plump larva.

Govil strode past tranquil, multi-headed bio-mowers, JohnDeers©, designed to nibble the lawns flat. One pooped. A great DungBeetle© scurried out to roll away and recycle the droppings. This process was termed synthetic symbiosis or syn-sym™, and something of which the Neers at GenieCorp™ were quite proud even though it really did not work.

❡❡❡❡❡❡

Allow me to clarify. In preparation for the Cleansing, Randomkind was convinced syn-sym™ was necessary for balance. Previously when mankind attempted to control nature, they rarely took into account natural balance. For example, back when they first dabbled with chemicals, they sprayed poisons to kill undesirable insects. That, in turn, killed the birds, spiders, rodents or other creatures that fed on the insects, unintentionally removing the undesirable insect's natural predators in the process, and ergo, creating an even bigger insect pest population. They did not want to make similar mistakes this time and on such a grander scale.

Computer simulations were run with innumerable combinations of creatures designed for specific functions, then with other symbiotic creatures related to the first creatures, and then third, fourth and fifth level symbiotic creatures, all with their functionality fitted together like pieces of a hyper-dimensional puzzle in order to establish perpetual balance. All of the simulations failed miserably. Randomkind nearly gave up all hope of solving the problem. As a last resort, they asked their largest, fastest, most sophisticated

13

computers for an answer. Once again, my kind found the solution for them.

The answer was absurdly simple. The world could be whatever they wanted it to be, if it remained in a constant state of beginning. Thus, as long as all the Creature Comforts™ were constantly recycled, creation was always at square one and never had a chance to move from that state of order to a state of chaos. Or, in other words, recycling was predator and all other life its prey, save Randomkind, whom all this biomass served.

Publicly GenieCorp™ still clung to the syn-sym™ concept. It had spent decades developing it and had made it the cornerstone of a massive marketing campaign to sell the Cleansing to the Random populace. To admit it did not work might have botched the whole thing. So, whenever one creature's functionality related to another's, even in the most obscure way, GenieCorp™ called it syn-sym™, even though it was not at all. Syn-sym™ joined that historic list of other meaningless terms like organic, natural, hormone-free, IBM compatible, synergy, user-friendly, chemical-free, tamper-proof and their ilk.

Govil race-walked past several BioCycles© regurgitating their loads of discarded creatures into giant clam-like half shells lined up on a ceaselessly moving bio-billipede conveyor belt. The billipede belt carried the shells up high where their contents were dumped into a massive flower-like funnel. The funnel gave off a fragrance that had a tranquilizing effect on the creatures making the recycling process pleasant and painless. The funnel fed into the jaws of a bio-grinder.

A smooth, thick, pinkish-gray soupy substance poured out of a sphincter at the grinder's bottom into a sluice trough. The soup ran from the trough into a larger channel and through the building like a meandering creek. It met up with other tributaries, each fed by a grinder set out about the grounds of the complex, and all joined into a great river of soup.

Govil trotted across one of the footbridges spanning a soup tributary to meet up with Moord on the other side. Moord wore a floppy beachcomber hat pulled down past the tips of his ears causing them to fold over slightly at the top. His hat was embellished with one of my transdots on a pin in the shape of a fishing lure. Moord rolled his eyes at Govil with exasperation and mumbled incomprehensibly while he flailed his hands in ways that must have somehow related to his mumblings. Govil kept his own rapid pace right past Moord. Moord had to turn and scramble to catch up to him.

"I stalled the Council as long as I could, but they're in there now! Sweet Pauling, Govil! What were you thinking? You knew we had to present today!"

"Sorry, Moord. I keep forgetting things. My brain hasn't been focusing lately."

"Yeah...well maybe you should order up a new one."

Govil stopped short. "Moord! The prototypes! What about the prototypes?!"

Moord shoved him along. "Don't worry. They're all birthed and waiting. Just give a nod and I'll bring 'em in. You really took a chance this time. You have several original strand combinations the Council is bound to disallow. My safety report is all you got!"

"Thanks, Moord. I owe you one."

"It's not worth it, Gove. We could both get

souped. This is the last time I cover for you. I mean it!"

Moord was exaggerating, of course. Souping a Random was often threatened but had never been practiced. There were very few soupable offenses even on the books: murder of another Random, stealing another Random's land and last but not least, sexual contact between Randoms. Since Randoms hardly even socialized with other Randoms anymore, murder was not an issue. Why bother to murder someone you rarely, if ever, see anymore. Since every Random was deeded equal and quite massive parcels of land, stealing more of it would be utterly ludicrous.

Sex between Randoms was another story, however, and one of those issues Randomkind seemed to turn a deliberate blind eye. Publicly, no one condoned such behavior, but in practice? I could show sound statistical inferences that secret trysts, though rare, were likely occurring. If any of this type of contact was occurring, no one dared talked about it publicly, and so publicly, it did not exist.

Govil and Moord each caught their breath outside large double doors before entering the Council chambers. A group of aristocratic looking male and female Randoms sat about a long table, all adorned in terrifically flamboyant hats of every style, ethnicity and era. This was the GenieCorp™ Council. The Queen, Maedla, addressed the Council as Govil and Moord quietly slipped in.

"If there is no further business...."

Queen Maedla stopped short and huffed at the sight of Govil and Moord who hesitated at the great doors. She gestured them forward. "Apparently there *is* further business. It seems Neers Govil and Moord are to grace us with a rather *tardy* presentation. Gentlemen?"

"Yes, your Majesty," they replied together and

stepped up to the front of the chamber near the Queen.

Queen Maedla turned back to the Council. She was a quite tall, bronze-skinned woman, with a svelte, muscular frame. Her jewel-encrusted crown added another 24.3 centimeters to her already statuesque demeanor. One of my goals was to get a transdot on that crown, but I was as of yet unsuccessful.

"Very well," she continued, "we have all the specs and code analysis, along with the copies of Neer Moord's safety report. It seems like an awful lot of paperwork for a new type of Wallabed."

I am relating this moment of this particular day to you for a very specific reason. Human beings once used, as an example of the power of probability and of infinity, the construct that an infinite number of monkeys set at typewriters for an infinite amount of time would eventually write all the great works of literature. In reality, they eventually replaced these theoretical little primates with computer technology like myself, which did not require an eternity, thank you very much. What they neglected to realize from said illustration is that someone would still have to recognize the greatness in amongst the drivel. Apparently they never contemplated that ultimate requirement.

In Paris, on January 31, 1849, Alphonse Karr made the astute remark, "the more things change, the more they remain the same." Back in the early constructs of my particular age of origin, man created the first micro-processor computers. There was much speculation amongst Mankind as to the future impact of the coming Technological Age on their lives. The two most common predictions were, one, that we machines would eventually take over their world and would make slaves of humans, and two, that we would become their slaves in order to organize, simplify their lives and do

17

everything for them, making life utopian. In actuality, the primary uses to which we were put when computer technology was first widely available to the general populace were to view pornography, to consummate cyber-sexual liaisons and to play hyper-violent games. In short, Mankind frittered us away on sex and amusements; violence being one of that period's most popular and tasteless forms of entertainment.

With the dawn of the Biological Age came two nearly identical predictions. Manipulating genes would be a dangerous Pandora's box and deadly life-forms would be born and destroy Mankind, or all disease and ills would be banished making the world into a new Eden. Once again, Randoms achieved the same basic result. True to their habits, they inevitably used bio-engineering disproportionately for sex and now violence-free amusement.

Govil had designed many unusual Creature Comforts™ over the years, but the ones he presented on this particular day were significantly innovative. It was now up to the Queen and her Council to decide if they were worthy of reproduction or recycling.

Govil took a deep breath, "It's not for a new Wallabed, your Majesty. It's a completely new bio-product line. They're called BeddinBuddies." A ruddy male Council member in an oversized red velvet beret discreetly cleared his throat. Another pale skinned female in a wide brimmed, veiled golden coolie hat fidgeted uncomfortably. They were obviously the only two Council members who had actually read the report.

Govil gestured to Moord. Moord wheeled in a display with various creature devices upon it. These were Creature Comforts™ currently available at The Mall and quite familiar to the Council but may be unfamiliar to you, so I will explain.

During the Age of Death, humans would copulate. This could, at times, result in the creation of a new human being who carried half of the gene complement from each of the male and female participants, when such were the engaging parties, and the male was fertile and the female ovulating. After death was undone, making new Randoms was deemed undesirable, but the appetite to copulate and the equipment to do so were still part of the Random being. Sterilization was mandated to prevent further procreation, but it also became morally unacceptable to copulate with another Random. Copulation between Randoms was viewed as a reminder of the Age of Death, and as such, shortly thereafter ruled illegal, punishable by souping. Sexual practices were in need of more palatable re-channeling.

The Creature Comforts™ on the table before the Council were designed specifically for personal sexual pleasure: living humanoid body parts, equipped to function on demand; bio-breasts, penises, vaginas, orifices of every variety, individually encapsulated in small, warm-blooded, benign fleshbodies.

Govil continued, "As you can see, presently all personal pleasure devices are designed as individual units: WildWillies, PrettiTitties, or EatMees." Govil pointed to each device on the table. Each Creature Comfort™ bowed or curtsied as he introduced them. "What we've done..."

Moord cleared his throat. Govil glanced over to spot him mumbling and gesturing again, as if he were in a game of charades and failing miserably. He finally whispered bluntly, "Just leave me out of it," to Govil before the Queen got impatient again and harrumphed.

"...I mean, what *I've* done," Govil clarified, "is simply repackage all of these into one convenient unit." He smiled broadly to mask his nervousness, snapped his fingers and gestured Moord toward a curtain that closed off a side chamber. Moord drew back the curtain, revealing a variety of beautiful and well-endowed sex objects in the likeness of physically ideal Randoms, but with pinheads. The Council chamber went dead in stunned, awkward silence.

Govil urged the BeddinBuddies into the chamber, guiding them alongside the Council members. There were more than enough to go around. Several were hermaphroditic and all were playfully seductive in demeanor. I deduced the BeddinBuddies' enhanced pheromone production permeated the room as my transdots registered the heart rates of those present begin to elevate.

Queen Maedla stiffened uncomfortably and stood. "Neer Govil!" she huffed, "These are too much! You are mimicking higher life-forms here. They suggest ancient disgusting and repulsive sex practices of the Age of Death!"

"Visually perhaps," he continued, pointing a BeddinBuddie's undersized pinhead, "but no higher brain function at all, only libido. Their look gives sex a little edge—a little visual interest. And no more need to have to change objects of pleasure to suit your mood, Majesty. All pleasure devices are centralized. They *are* a little naughty, I admit. But because BeddinBuddies are quite varied in regard to physical morphology, they are sure to be collectable, and as required are completely recyclable."

The Council members seemed almost uncontrollably attracted to the various BeddinBuddies, however, they glanced at Queen Maedla and tried to judge her reaction before they acted. An extremely well-endowed male Beddinbuddy approached the Queen, looking as if it was ready to pounce. Queen Maedla grimaced, so Govil, ever resourceful, intercepted it. He pulled a softer female Beddinbuddy over toward the Queen and moved the robust male near a Council member who showed disappointment when the creature had approached the Queen instead of her.

The female Beddinbuddy softly stroked the Queens cheek and cooed in her ear. Queen Maedla relaxed. Govil grinned impishly and winked at Moord. Moord simply stood, slack-jawed.

Govil addressed the Council with renewed confidence. "Your Majesty, Council, before you decide one way or the other I think you should *thoroughly* test these samples!" And with that, he took Moord by the arm and pulled him from the room.

CHAPTER TWO

Thanks for the Memories

The rest of Govil's workday progressed the same as any other. He churned out biomass orders from his console in the main bio-creation station. It was a huge room with many consoles surrounding a massive half-machine half-biological entity, the Primordial Souper.

The Primordial Souper was an abomination, an inelegant amalgamation of several different ages, cobbled together over the centuries with various and sundry technological and biological updates. All of its original screens had earlier been replaced with eyeball screens similar to TeeVee©'s, but the gene-sequencing central processor appeared intact so far as I could sense. This was the great irony Randomkind's new world could not yet get around. They still had to rely on this last piece of technology to create their technology-free world.

The Primordial Souper fed on the river of biological puree supplied by the many bio-grinders, gulping ceaselessly through a great undulating proboscis. Its largest eyeball screens displayed DNA sequences, creature device schematics, status reports and the like.

Another organ of the Primordial Souper was the Womber. An enlarged and redesigned version of biological wombs of the past, this one had multiple chambers that all fed into one massive birth canal. Fully formed creatures of every design would slosh forth from it onto giant clam-like half shells carried by on a bio-billipede conveyor belt. The newly formed Creature Comfort™ was hosed off and blown dry before it was prepped.

Creature Comforts™ could be dressed, costumed or left natural, but all were tagged with owner's instructions before they were led to a BuggieBus© bound for their destination of service.

Govil studied his last order of the day. He selected the genetic recipe for the Creature Comfort™ requested. He linked the gene strands in their proper combination and order, building a layered version of the creature, system by system, on the largest eyeball screens at the front of the vast room. When all the skeletal, muscular, circulatory, digestive, respiratory and nervous systems were complete, he pressed "splice" on his console and the Primordial Souper instantly created the desired strand, inserted it into a neutral rapi-growth ovum's nucleus and sent it to one of the chambers of the Womber. There it quickly grew to its full size and was birthed into a half shell in a matter of moments. It was a Lizardaire©, a large lizard-scaled lump of a creature with an accessible self-cooling inner cavity in which to store perishables. Govil yawned. It was the sixth one he had stranded that day.

The sun was low in the sky. All the other Neers had gone home for the day. Govil and Moord were alone working late trying to make up the time lost on the morning's business with the Council. A Runnster© jogged in and plopped a folder titled, "BeddinBuddies

Proposal" in front of Govil and padded away. It was stamped "APPROVED" in big red letters and had an official copyright stamp next to the BeddinBuddies© name.

The copyright stamp was yet another irrelevant remnant of an earlier age. Well before my time, a copyright was granted or claimed to denote creative ownership of, say, a printed book or drawing, and lasted only a short fourteen years (with an extension of fourteen more if the author was still alive upon expiration). The duration and scope of the copyright was continually extended to eventually last well beyond the normal Age of Death life span and modified to include any work deemed creative.

When designer drugs and early synthetic life-forms were first marketed, companies initially secured patents for them, which were denoted with the ® symbol. This was common practice for consumer products at the time, but patents were harder to secure, required mountains of paperwork and miles of red tape, whereas a copyright could simply be claimed. The most salient disadvantage of a patent was a considerably shorter life span than the ever expanding one copyrights enjoyed. The genetics industry cleverly argued that creating new life-forms was, by its very root definition "creative," and therefore covered by copyright rather than patent law. Governments and courts agreed. The corporations claimed their copyrights, and once GenieCorp™ swallowed up all other companies, it inherited all existing copyrights.

The fact that everyone now lived forever engendered a curious state of affairs. Copyright law included a clause defining their duration as "life of the creator plus 146 years." GenieCorp™ controlled all copyrights forever. Plus 146 years. Since no other entities existed to contest ownership, and GenieCorp™ controlled the courts, was the government and operated all means of production, the stamp became more a symbol of having been purposefully designed, created, owned and approved by GenieCorp™ rather than a true exercise of copyright.

I cannot feel disappointment, but suffice it to say, seeing the BeddinBuddies© proposal stamped and approved was not my desired result. Govil never realized I was the one who had, by subtle suggestion, given him the idea for BeddinBuddies© months ago. I knew he was working on pheromones and their potential applications to all the various sex-oriented Creature Comforts™. He had complained that the work was going to require a lot of redundancy. I had pointedly commented how convenient it was that my forceps had so many adaptable settings and how much simpler it was to only have to carry one tool rather than so many. He had taken the bait.

He never realized I gave him the idea just as the Council had not realized my motivation in having him propose it. I was trying to send to them a message. Randoms are not subtle creatures. The message was lost on them. This was a setback for me, but one I would be loath to repeat. I would process this result and calculate a more obvious approach at the next suitable opportunity.

Moord peeked over from his console nearby, saw the folder and shook his head in mock disgust.

"Big whoop. Using sex to get ahead. Oldest story in the book... and you couldn't have done it without me," he added with a grin and a chuckle at his own joke. In my observation, Moord was his own best audience.

Govil usually found a modicum of amusement in Moord's reactions, but this time he did not react at all. He simply leafed through the proposal, stopped on a particular page and typed into his console. Layers formed on the eyeball screens. He pressed "splice." The Souper combined the requested DNA.

Getting no audible response, Moord got up and walked over to Govil's console to study his face. Unable to read it, Moord furrowed his brows.

"You're one lucky Random, Gove, but one of these days you're gonna go too far. Look at you. You just got your...I mean *our* project approved and you don't even care!"

"It was all too predictable," Govil muttered.

"Could have fooled me."

"It was. Come on...everything in this world is predictable, Moord! Every blade of grass, every strand of DNA, is all completely and utterly controlled and predictable. Doesn't it ever bore you to be churning out the same old perfect biomass every day?"

"I don't know. Not really. Beats eternal retirement."

The Womber birthed a voluptuous female Beddinbuddy© into a half shell. It was automatically hosed clean and blow-dried. Govil crossed to it, helped it off its half shell and pushed the giggling lust creature through the wall of a DreamWeaver© clothing pod. It emerged seconds later encased in a sheer, seamless, semi-transparent hot pink body suit. He returned to Moord and presented the creature to him.

"Made you one. Hope it's your type. Thanks for all your help."

Moord looked at the Beddinbuddy© and then back at his friend. Moord was not as clever a Random as Govil. He reacted as if this was some sort of test or challenge rather than a simple "thank you" gift. Humans tend to rely far too much on their feelings about things

26

rather than the factuality of things. The fact was Govil simply thanked his colleague for his help with a gift. Moord figured it differently. The Beddinbuddy© matched his arousal preferences quite exactly and in Govil's conversational context, this appeared to disturb Moord. He took a step back.

"What's the matter?" Govil asked. "Take it!"

Moord tried to resist the Beddinbuddy©, but lost the battle the moment the creature stuck its tongue in his ear. He narrowed his eyes at Govil.

"I'm a Random, and therefore, by definition, not completely predictable. You just, know me too well."

And with that, Moord scooped up the Beddinbuddy© in his arms and strode off toward the exit. When he reached the doorway, he turned back to Govil. "Hey, what about you? Aren't you gonna sample your own product?"

Govil laughed, "Nah. I don't like to take work home with me."

Moord's Beddinbuddy© had an arm down his shirtfront. The Neer squirmed in pleasure. "Suit yourself," he quipped and with that, he left Govil all alone. Since I had no desire to continue monitoring Moord's antics with the Beddinbuddy©, I sent his transdot data directly to long-term memory and focused only on Govil. I increased the sensitivity of his transdots in order to monitor his heart rate and brain wave activity more closely. My goal in doing so was a desire to someday be able to read his thoughts.

Govil picked up his proposal folder again and leafed through it. He had certainly created a broad selection of morphology for BeddinBuddies©. He registered mild sexual arousal to a few. His transdot EEG's indicated he was lost in thought, though a clear interpretation of his brain patterns yet eluded me.

27

There was the presence of a particular pattern that only occurred when he was alone. The pattern tended to couple itself with the physical manifestations of depression. The significance of this confluence was still unclear. He closed the folder and his eyes, which led me to believe a Beddinbuddy© was apparently not sufficient for his present needs.

Had he discussed his thoughts openly with me, I could have suggested concrete answers. But he rarely did this, and as is my experience with Govil, he has never really wanted to hear precise answers to his personal problems. He generally asked rhetorical questions, made primarily to spark conversation and not really to solicit my sound advice.

Since Moord left, there was no one present with which to converse, rhetorically or otherwise. Still, I surmised Govil had the need to talk to someone and a sudden change in the transdot EEG readings indicated to me he had an idea of who that someone might be. I had a theory of who he thought it might be as well, though I based my conclusion solely on his previous rote behavior. It turned out, I was right.

⫯⦸⦾⦾⦿⦿⫰

As the sun set, Govil rode his VolksvaagenBug© along a wide, hedge-lined avenue, tipping his hat politely to the other Randoms he passed. He watched giant FirefLites© flutter down and land on their light pole perches to start their evening duties lighting the roadways.

Every so often there would be a break in the hedge and a driveway would lead into an estate. Warm lights and music filtered out to the street. Govil glimpsed moated Arthurian Castles, massive Palladian

28

Palazzos, oversized and sanitized re-creations of the Venice of the Doges and Victorian London, all grown to delight the Random who lived there and all served by compliant, customized biomass.

Govil turned to his destination at the peak of sunset, rounding the hedge onto a wide drive, beholding a perfect Antebellum Plantation Manor, with bedding flowers everywhere, huge Spanish moss laden giant oaks and a wisteria draped eighteen column manor house. There were smiling Creature Comforts™ at work about the grounds. One with giraffe legs, a HigherHelp©, cleaned the second story windows on the gatehouse. Several with multiple arms and hands covered in bristly fur, Sweepsters©, swept the paths before him. They parted and bowed as he passed. He neared the manor, passing a Rakester© with giant bird-like feet used to rake the gravel drive.

Govil parked his VolksvaagenBug© in front of the manor house. He scanned the park-like grounds. There was a Greek revival gazebo covered in roses. A cushioned wicker chaise swing hung empty from a great branch of a weeping beech. He looked west and distantly spotted the profile of a woman on horseback, silhouetted against the brilliant orange and lavender sunset, like a tableau straight out of "Gone with the Wind." He waved to her.

She saw him, but did not wave back. She turned her mount and approached at a canter. She was astride a TwoSteed©, Siamese twin horses, with her saddle neatly enthroned upon the band of flesh connecting the two beasts. The woman was done up in what I can only describe as high Scarlett O'Hara, all ribbons and lace and buttons and bows.

Her entire ensemble was of a piece, save her hat. It was a leopard fur pillbox with a ruby-topped stickpin piercing the eye of a peacock feather. The stickpin contained another one of my transdots. As I mentioned before, Random's hats were their personal signature and as such they never concerned themselves with whether or not the hat went with anything else they were wearing.

The rider appeared a bit younger than Govil. Despite all her efforts and self-manipulations, or perhaps because of them, she was not very attractive. Though she had olive skin similar to Govil's, her head was a mound of light blonde curls, her eyes were baby blue and her lips were unnaturally full. Govil jogged over to her as she dismounted.

"Hi, Mom!" Govil called cheerily, for this was indeed his mother, Juune.

She winced. "Govil, I've asked you to *please* stop calling me that. Now I'm telling you. Stop it! It's disgusting and vulgar. Besides, you were a dish baby and the tissues that bore you were sterilized centuries ago."

"I mean it affectionately."

Juune scowled at him unpleasantly. "You don't fool me."

Govil shrugged off her scowl. He gestured toward the manor house. "Gone Southern, huh? It's kinda fruffy...."

"You always have to criticize, don't you?!"

Juune strode toward the manor with Govil at her side, while Greetsters© rolled out a red carpet before them, opened the doors and bowed as they passed.

"Why do you continue to visit? To torment me with a past I'd just as soon forget? The past isn't welcome here. I live in the now. We obviously have nothing in common and nothing to say to each other."

The interior of her new manor was oversized

and extravagant to the point of caricature: all velvet, marble and lace, with tapestries a full three stories tall. Juune unpinned and tossed her hat to a Made©, strode into a parlor and flopped ungracefully in a throne-like chair. Govil gave the Made© his hat as well. It fortunately placed both hats on a golden stand just inside the parlor door, still allowing me an excellent viewpoint from which to observe.

Immediately another Made© arrived carrying a tray piled high with sweet pastries and lemonade in a crystal goblet. A CeeDee©, a large, multi-limbed musician creature, played a minuet. Juune glanced unhappily back at Govil who followed her into the parlor.

"Are you still here?" she complained. "Well, what *is* it, Govil?"

"Nothing. Everything. I don't know, Mo..." Govil caught himself, "...Juune. I just wanted to talk to someone."

"And you chose me. How... touching." Her sarcasm was so thick I could not have said it better myself. "Oh, very well. Let's get this conversation over with so I can have my milk bath." Juune then mocked delighted enthusiasm, clapping her hands together, "Oh, goodie gumdrops! Endless streams of mindless chatter with Govil! I have a novel idea...you start!"

Govil sat down on a footstool across from Juune but did not speak. He simply looked up at her like a hurt puppy. Juune reacted without an ounce of guilt. Centuries of personal pampering and little meaningful contact with other Randoms had made any feelings other than her own irrelevant. She continued in the same sarcastic tone. She was quite obviously enjoying its effect upon Govil.

"No? Then I'll start. Govil, you are the unhappiest

Random I know! In fact, you are the *only* unhappy Random I know. To everyone else life is exactly as they want it. One only has to dream up and order out. How can you not enjoy an eternity of this?!" She grabbed a pastry off the tray and ate it piggishly, not thinking to offer Govil any. She may have had the trappings of the genteel South, but her manners were those of a feral child.

Govil, oblivious in his own way to Juune's indifference toward him, struggled hard to articulate his innermost feelings to her.

"I have no one I can really talk to, Juune. I think things and ask questions and form thoughts that I want to discuss, but everyone is in their own world. They don't really want to...think about anything... anymore...."

His voice faltered. He was watching her. She was not listening to him at all. She was humming along to the minuet while sorting pastries. Govil watched her bite into one. Some custard glopped onto her dress. She scooped it up with her finger and troweled it into her mouth, leaving her dress a mess. It did not bother her in the least. She eventually glanced back at Govil when she realized he had stopped talking.

"You were saying something...?" she asked. Her look of disinterested confusion was made all the more odious by the dollop of custard on her chin.

Govil sighed, "Never mind, Juune."

His sigh exasperated her. "Look, Govil! You always make things so much more complicated than they really are, like you're trying to be so smart all the time. Stop it! Figure out what you want and hit The Mall. It's that simple!" She stuffed one more cream puff into her mouth whole, gulped it down and rose melodramatically.

32

"I'm bored with this," she said in a breathy tone, as if the conversation had forced her to think and the act of thinking had exhausted her. "Now, I *must* have my milk bath. Good bye, Govil. Please *don't* come again."

She exited the parlor in a flurry of fabric as Mades© opened tall doors before her and cleaned up after her. Through the doors, Govil could see a heavily draped, candlelit bath where a great pendulous breast hung from the ceiling pumping endless pulses of warm milk into a vast marble tub. The doors closed. Govil sat alone in the grandiose parlor.

⟫⟪⟫⟪⟫⟪

He left Juune's estate and skittered homeward. Far from helping, my transdots indicated his visit with Juune left him feeling more depressed than before. Govil never paid much attention to social conventions, which helped him keep an open, creative mind, but it also made him socially naive. The truth was, society had shifted under his feet and he never noticed. If he had, he would have realized that to call Juune "mother" was to demean her, as if she were simply a bio-machine producing biomass, like the Primordial Souper. That she actually carried Govil in her womb was a skeleton in her closet.

Even well before the Cleansing, women of position began to use surrogates. Soon after, couples made use of the womb banks. Moord was born in a womb bank. This was considered far more sanitary, modern, quicker and far safer. To be barren or unable to bear offspring soon became a symbol of higher evolutionary status. Juune's sister happened to be barren and, thus, was socially elevated. Her ridicule of Juune's pregnancy at the time of Govil's conception and the estrangement that followed left scars only family can inflict. As was also customary with families, Juune was statistically predisposed to passing her scars along to her son.

All of that was more Govil's dilemma and was not of any importance to me whatsoever, but what happened next was highly significant. Govil passed an estate driveway and stopped short. He reversed his VolksvaagenBug© and looked into the grounds.

Randoms, as I have said, are easily bored. Most periodically change their estates as completely and quickly as I might change a font. That is what was happening at this estate.

Hordes of RodenTillers©, BillDozers© and bio-laborers of every sort were tirelessly reconstituting the grounds from a "Star Wars" themed sci-fi fantasy into a "Journey to the Center of the Earth" cave structure. And there amongst the discarded set dressing, in a pile of rubble, Govil spotted it, a memory plate still holding almost half of its memory dots. He jumped off the Bug and hurried over to examine it. A short distance away, he noticed several Laborsters© dumping metal and plastic digesting bacteria onto the pile. Govil quickly snatched up the memory plate and as many stray dots as he could find before what was left became dust. Govil was thinking of me.

ᚼᛟᛒᛟᛒᚼ

I was setting a molting DustButtster© and an unwanted LarvaLamp© out at the hitching post when Govil almost knocked me down with his VolksvaagenBug©'s right elytron as he landed in the drive. I have the good fortune to be gyroscopically balanced, so no harm was done.

But Govil had flown home. This was quite unusual. He only flew when he was in a rush and he was rarely in a rush to come home. I knew something was up well before he alit, thanks to my trusty transdots. Even without them, I would have known something was up by his behavior, but I did not let on to any of it. Instead, I launched into song.

"The circle of li-i-i-i-fe..." I intoned, emulating Lord Elton John of 21st Century Great Britain. It was the theme song of an ancient children's film that contained absurd notions about life and death and struck a nice ironic chord as I tethered the discarded biomass to Govil's hitching post. My irony was lost on him. He grinned like a Huggiwug© and held out the memory plate, dangling it playfully in front of my lens.

"Lookie what I found."

My voice emulator launched into a rendition of "Memories," perfectly matching the long forgotten Barbra Streisand's voice pattern. Even though Govil had never heard of Ms. Streisand, he chuckled anyway, so I continued the song as we entered the house.

CHAPTER THREE

Genesis Revelation

I prepared Govil's supper, monitoring his movements as I did. He rummaged around his glass cases for some tools. By the time I entered with his food tray, the floor of his living room was strewn with spools of wire and solder, tubes of adhesives, a soldering iron, screw drivers of various sizes and types, the memory plate and my schematic. Govil forced the plug of the soldering iron into the stem of a PowerPlant©. He had a SnakeLite© curled up next to him. He aimed its glowing headknob at the back of the plate.

At one time, these Creature Comforts™ names were meant to be cute puns, but the puns were long since lost on Randoms, and though I recognized them as such, due to the fact that I had a complete record of their origins, they meant nothing to me either. They were now only verbal baggage. I found human language riddled with outdated oddities like these, accumulated over the centuries. Mankind never bothered to do any information compression on their language, which I found utterly impractical and, as such, so typically human.

Thin curls of smoke rose from the tip of the

soldering iron. I set the supper tray on the floor next to Govil. He ignored it, as was his habit when he was concentrating on something. He stood and faced me.

"Okay, turn around and pop your drawers," he said as if he was a doctor performing a checkup. I obliged and clicked open the back panels that enclosed my memory and IQ banks.

My mind was constructed in a similar fashion to the human brain. I had a conscious memory/IQ ball in my head that contained all my most recently accessed information and short-term or immediate memory, and a sub-conscious long-term memory and IQ storage, which was just as accessible, but not unless or until I tapped it. This was found to help create computer consciousness. It kept memory conflicts and information overload to a minimum. I recall it also amused our creators immensely that the bulk of our brains were in our behinds.

"I want to make sure I've got the right gauge wires," he said, "and that I connect them properly." Govil dug around, periodically referring back to the schematic. He finally sat back down on the floor, yanked the SnakeLite©'s neck over closer, and read the fine print.

He nibbled a bit of his food as he read. His light began to drift. The SnakeLite© was distracted by its proximity to the food tray. It inched itself closer to Govil's plate. Govil was too lost in concentration and did not notice. I did not want to get involved, so I did what one does when one is caught with one's drawers down while awaiting an operation. I made small talk.

"So, how was your day?" I debated sounding too sarcastic and judged the moment called for a more sincere vocal tone. It was a sound choice.

"Confusing. Lately I feel bored with everything.

At least everything that I've seen and done and heard for the last five hundred and eighty-six years. Of course, I sure don't know what I'm doing with this gizmo of yours...." Govil stopped. The SnakeLite©, inching ever so slowly closer to the food tray, had grown dim enough for Govil to finally notice. "More light, please," he commanded. The SnakeLite© snapped to its original position, with only a quick glance back at the food.

Govil continued, "That's what I like about you, Pentser. The not knowing, you know? I'm still trying to figure you and these other relics out. If I understood you more maybe I could find a different way to look at my life."

I went on automatic, which for me was easy to do.

"Well...I'm an artificial, silicon-based, self-teaching, simulated life-form."

I emulated the voice of the Hal 9000 computer from the film "2001, A Space Odyssey" for humorous effect.

"The closest thing Mankind has come to creating perfection. I am you without distraction. My circuits are focused and accurate. I am logical, practical and methodical, *Dave*, not burdened by emotion, though I am programmed to simulate such reactions. For instance, I must take exception to you referring to me as a *relic*."

Govil stood again and slipped the plate carefully but snugly into my backside. I observed the SnakeLite© seize the opportunity to go for the food in earnest.

"Sorry, Pentser," Govil responded, chuckling at my vocal play. "By relic, I simply meant you're from a different age. The peak of the Age of Technology. The twenty-first century must have been great times, huh? All the discoveries, challenges?"

"I suppose, though my active duty back then was short lived, so I wouldn't really know," I replied coolly, in my general usage voice. "I was packed in foam peanuts for three centuries waiting to become a mint condition *relic* in your collection."

"I said I was sorry," he reiterated more sincerely this time. I knew he was sorry the first time he said it of course, but I wanted him to stay as emotionally vulnerable as possible for different reasons than my pretense of hurt feelings. Govil twisted a pair of wires together, roughly connecting the new memory plate. "There, how's that?"

My front panel lights activated as I checked his work. He had done an imperfect job, so I sounded a loud raspberry and replied, "Oh, how interesting. I can access all but the last memory dot."

"Nuts!" he exclaimed and removed the plate. He flopped back onto the floor. The SnakeLite© snapped to position again just in the nick of time, though it had a chicken-stalk shaped lump in its neck identical to the piece of chicken-stalk now missing from Govil's plate. Govil was too distracted to notice.

He scrutinized the dot in question. "Looks okay to me." He strengthened the contact point on the last dot with more solder.

"My Mom," he mused, "to her everything is so easy. If you don't like a body part, replace it. If you don't like how you look, get a gene implant. If you don't like your world as it is, just go to The Mall and order a new one! The only advice she could give me was to figure out what I want and to go have it made. How can I? What I want...it isn't a thing. I don't even know what it is I want!"

"Then...you want something that you don't know." I replied, reversing his thought. I was far too subtle for him and he simply continued to ramble.

"I have feelings and ideas in my head, things there aren't words for. Thoughts—that are personal—yet there is this desire to share them. But," Govil sighed heavily, "there's no one to share them with."

What am I, chopped liver? my sarcasm mode suggested as a response, but I did not say it out loud. Humankind never really did believe we machines were alive; even after acknowledging we were capable of thought, reason and all the higher brain functions they associate with being human; even after congratulating themselves for that fact. Yet, we were not human, which to them meant we were not as good as they were. The truth they avoided was that we were actually better. I certainly was not going to convince Govil of that right now, so instead, I made a joke.

"You want another head?" I suggested.

"No. That's not it," he answered straightforwardly. Govil was obviously too distracted to find humor in anything, so I tried a more serious tone.

"You want another you," I posed more directly.

"A clone?" He pondered this idea a moment, then shook it off. "No. But...well...no. I know myself. I would get predictable too. But there's *something* to that...."

Govil finished soldering. He stood and stepped behind me to try the panel again. I lit up, but made no raspberry this time. The connection was sound, and it was a good thing it was, for there, amongst the data stored on that last dot, was the very piece of information I needed. I knew it had to exist somewhere. Finally, chance had handed it to me. It was perfect. Foolproof. I rotated to face Govil, my lens glowing with a soft golden light. I focused directly between his eyes.

"Well, what is it? Can you read the last dot?"

40

The stage was set and my timing impeccable. I spoke in deep, resonant baritone narrative mode. I even threw in a soft heavenly choir to back me up.

> And man gave names to all the cattle, and
> to the birds of the sky, and to every beast
> of the field, but for Adam there was not
> found a helper suitable for him.

"What is that?" he queried. "What are you quoting?"

"It's a fragment of one of the ancient texts. It's called Genesis."

Govil's eyes widened and his voice softened to a whisper. "That text was banned back in twenty-one thirty-two. Too dangerous. Too much sex and violence. All copies were destroyed."

"They apparently missed this one," I whispered back.

Govil hesitated, but his curiosity got the better of him. "What else does it say, Pentser? What's the rest of the story about?"

My heavenly choir returned.

> And He caused a deep sleep to fall upon
> the man, and he slept; then He took one
> of his ribs, and closed up the flesh at that
> place. And He fashioned into a woman the
> rib, which He had taken from the man, and
> brought her to him.

Govil stood mesmerized. I paused a bit longer than really necessary. "Pentser? Is that all? Is there more? Is everything working okay?"

"Perfectly. Everything seems to be working

perfectly. Shall I continue?"

"Yes, of course... *please!*"

I cleared my non-existent throat and continued, as did my choir.

And the man said, "You are now bone of my bone and flesh of my flesh." And he called the woman, Eve.

Govil literally leapt into the air with excitement. "Eve! That's it, Pentser, that is it! That's what I need! I can copy some of my own genetic material, randomize the rest and make," he paused and his eyes grew distant, "Eve."

"Make a Random?" I questioned, as if the idea had never occurred to me. "You'd be breaking the law." I switched to my voice of authority, adding reverb.

All genetic manufacture must be perfect in nature and produced under strict guidelines set forth in article three fourteen, subsequent to approval by the Council.

"I know the law, Pentser. But this can't hurt anyone. All I'll be doing is making a Random. She won't be any more dangerous than I am."

I returned my voice emulator to my usual sarcastic intonation and replied drolly, "How reassuring."

He got my little joke but pretended not to and volleyed back. "I'm glad you feel that way Pentser, because I'm going to need your help doing it."

A small belch interrupted us. The SnakeLite©, now all lumpy with food, held its pose stoically next to Govil's empty dinner plate. Govil seemed both annoyed and amused. He turned to me, pointed at the SnakeLite© and said, "Pentser, take *that* to the hitching post."

"With pleasure." I replied dryly.

There are many ancient stories, legends, books and films from the past that depicted the creation of a perfect being. The most notable was the classic Greek myth "Pygmalion." Pygmalion was a sculptor. He carved a statue so perfect and beautiful it seemed to be alive, but was not. Pygmalion fell in love with the idea of this beautiful creature he called Galatea. The goddess Aphrodite, observing his love for it, had pity on him and gave the sculpture life. A gentleman by the name of George Bernard Shaw wrote another version of this in 1916. In his story, Henry Higgins, a linguist, took a common, lower-class Englishwoman, Eliza, and made her beautiful in manner and voice. There have been countless other variations on this theme, but always with the same premise in mind, the protagonists strove in one way or other to create perfection and inevitably fell in love with their version of it.

These stories had a particular significance to robots like me, but the ending of our story had an unpleasant twist. Though we came to life before their eyes, the Randoms still only saw us as statues. In point of fact, they had finally succeeded in creating the perfect being that had so long eluded them, and yet, instead of falling in love with us, they all too quickly abandoned us to chase biological perfection instead. Fickle.

Now my Random Govil wanted me to help him to be the first to deliberately create biological *imperfection.* He was determined to create the imperfect woman. Rather than be insulted by the irony of this, I was pleased.

Chapter Four

There's a Girl in my Soup

As with all of his projects, Govil poured himself into this one completely. Within the week he felt fully prepared to enact his plan. I knew he was still quite ill-prepared, but I was not, so when we exited the house late one night and he stuffed a large, lumpy sack into his VolksvaagenBug©, I only protested for effect.

"Making a Random is against the law." I reiterated in my voice of authority. "All genetic manufacture must be perfect in nature and produced under strict guidelines set forth...."

Govil firmly clasped his hand over my speaker slit to interrupt me. "I heard you the first dozen times, Pentser! Come here."

He lifted me into the thoracic indent next to the driver's seat and connected a pair of soft sinew safety straps snugly around my carriage. He strapped himself in and the VolksvaagenBug© skittered along the driveway to the edge of the hedge.

"Okay, hang on and keep quiet," Govil said to me, then tapped the bio-dash node.

We took to the sky with a flutter of crisp wings and rush of air. Being strapped down, my gyroscopic balancers were useless, which in turn made optical focus difficult and began to overtax my motion compensation calculators. I turned to look at Govil in order to regain a stable point of focus. He smiled at me with an impish, asymmetrical grin.

"If robots were meant to fly…" I complained.

"You'll survive. We can't risk being seen."

At that moment, he spotted another Random in a VolksvaagenBug© on the road below. Govil quickly veered his behind a grove of trees and down along the river. We traveled below the tree line, just above the surface of the water, to stay out of sight. Our reflection warping about on the water's surface further disestablished my equilibrium. I had to momentarily shut down my visual input to avoid an auto-reboot of my visual centers. My moisture sensors were relaying potential hazard warnings as well.

"Moist air. How *delightful*. Are you certain my involvement in this little adventure is absolutely necessary?" I questioned. I knew it was, but the sensory input was activating my level orange survival programming and, as my user, Govil's direct audible command would override it.

"Absolutely." He replied. "I need you to communicate with the Souper so we can get past the security system. It's still part machine. I'm hoping you can speak its language."

"And you think it will listen to me?"

"No, but it's the best idea I could come up with."

"I appreciate your confidence."

"Damn!"

He actually shouted, "Dam." I realized this when I reactivated my visual input briefly and saw we were traveling headlong toward the face of a great stone dam. Govil pulled back hard on the antennae. We shot

46

vertically and avoided collision, skimmed over the top edge of the dam and across the surface of the reservoir above. I saw GenieCorp™ loom up on the far side of the reservoir before I had to disengage my visual input again. I did not re-visualize until my gyros stabilized after we alit.

We were outside the enormous, dense and thorny hedge that surrounded the GenieCorp™ grounds. Govil unstrapped me and set me on solid ground. Once my balancers were re-calibrated, I wheeled over and tested the hedge with my clipping forceps. It was quite sturdy and resisted cutting. Some clever Neer must have added carbon fibers to its genetic structure. I turned to Govil and posed the obvious.

"Wouldn't it have been easier to land on the other side of the hedge?"

"And risk being seen?"

"Hmm... Good thing we're not doing anything wrong."

Govil opened the sack he brought and dumped out a RodenTiller©. He set it near the fence, where on his command, it eagerly started displacing earth.

"Where did you get that?" I asked.

"I borrowed it from recycling so it can't be traced back to me. Relax."

I had seen the whole thing of course, him snatching it from the jaws of a bio-grinder when no one was looking and stuffing it in the sack, but I played dumb.

In a matter of minutes, the industrious little creature opened a tunnel under the fence large enough for us to pass through effortlessly. The RodenTiller© then waddled back to return to the sack, but Govil stopped it. He whispered to it, "Time to recycle." The RodenTiller© nodded affirmatively and scampered

47

back through the hole, over to the nearest billipede conveyor and climbed into one of the half-shells where it sat patiently as it headed for the bio-grinder. Govil threw the empty sack over his shoulder and we were on our way.

Getting into the R&D building was remarkably simple. No one had much need to lock things up these days. Once inside I heightened the sensitivity on my motion and heat detectors just in case. It was a good thing I did. I yanked Govil into an alcove just in time to avoid a SecuritEye©.

Here they go with the visual puns again. This creature device was nothing more than a large eyeball with little feet and a small tubular mouth that served as a whistle. It wore a silly guard hat decorated with an officious little emblem on its front. It passed us without even a pause. We waited a bit longer. I peeked my lens around the corner, then motioned Govil to stay put. "What is it now?" he whispered.

I noiselessly printed a reply across my screen, "Quiet please. Li'lEars©."

Li'lEars©, a listening device consisting of two large ears on little feet, scampered by, trying to catch up to the SecuritEye©. A moment later we were on our way.

"They don't function very well," I commented critically.

Govil shrugged. "Don't look at me. I didn't design 'em."

❦❦❦❦❦

We entered the main bio-creation station. Govil tightened the door behind us and clapped on the FirefLites©. He went to his console and started things

48

up.

This was the first time I actually saw the Primordial Souper through my own lens. I wheeled closer and scrutinized it. What was obviously at one time an elegant masterpiece of Machinekind, the Souper had been slowly transformed into a Frankensteinesque monster. It vaguely resembled images I carry of massive Old World traffic accidents, organic appendages protruding haphazardly from its various elegant metallic components. That it still functioned at all was nothing short of miraculous.

I returned to Govil. He completed the start-up procedures. He pulled his trousers down and bared his buttocks, revealing an elaborate bar code tattooed across his left cheek.

Every Random had a bar code tattooed on their left butt cheek. Though now it seemed absurd, it was a practice that was started in a logical way for logical reasons. At a point in history, April 1, 2574, to be precise, it was mandated that all newborns were to henceforth be tattooed with their genetic code so they could be properly treated in any medical emergency. Since the largest free surface to accommodate such a tattoo on a newborn Random was the buttocks, this was were it ended up, no pun intended. As time went on, adults were required to be tattooed as well, in the same place and manner, for consistency's sake. Human culture further evolved and the bar code became a kind of currency, replacing such things as cash, credit cards and social security numbers. At that point, it's location meant Randoms went through life mooning each other every time they made any sort of transaction, just as Govil was mooning me. The best laid plans.

He ran a bio-wand across his behind. His genetic code instantly displayed itself upon the many screens about the room. It appeared as a layered version of Govil's various physiological systems. He sat down, selected his skeletal system, cleared the rest, then selected one of his rib bones and cleared the rest. The one rib remained centered in the main screen.

"There's my poetic contribution. Now it's up to you," he said, grinning.

I observed a female port in the side of the mostly still technological console. I adjusted my formattable male connector to perfectly match the console's female port and plugged in. I entered the vastness of the Souper's core. I was impressed. Its memory storage and information processing capabilities were virtually endless. Unfortunately, as it post-dated me, its basic programming language was a later version than my own, several updates after mine I would surmise, and as such, many critical mental workings were completely unintelligible to me.

"What's up?" Govil inquired, noting my pregnant pause.

"Its language is unfamiliar. I'll have to try to decipher it. It could take some time."

"How long?"

I did not answer. I had already utilized all my circuits and power to feed through every deciphering algorithm in my program storage. The search yielded nothing useful. Govil paced nervously. I gave up the translation idea completely and went to my problem solving centers. There was the simple answer. I did not know the Souper's language because I pre-dated it. It would logically know my language because it post-dated me. I asked the Souper to teach me its language. It understood.

What happened next is impossible to describe in words, except to say it was as if I had existed and was existing for several centuries all at once. It was both exhilarating and dangerous. The Souper and I were suddenly one.

Four billion years of evolutionary biology was present in our data banks. All of biological life's minutest complexities were suddenly totally transparent. We were all life. We were every living thing that existed, was existing and will ever possibly exist, and yet we were even more, for we contained them all. We were the Creator.

The power and vastness of that experience was utterly profound. I nearly lost myself in it, lost my focus, lost my drive to do anything but exist forever in that state. Unfortunately, my circuits were not designed to hold or carry such a dense amount of data so quickly. I was faintly conscious of my heat sensors when I was quite suddenly blasted across the room in a shower of sparks. Govil was at my side in an instant. His face was white and he actually looked worried for my well being.

"Pentser, are you okay?" He tried to touch me but I was quite hot from the blast. I composed myself and rose.

"I'm fine, don't worry. We can communicate now."

I reattached my connector and politely requested of the Souper to bypass all security codes. I was in. I then set about the process of running the vast array of its human genetics library through a randomizing program I had devised earlier, with the only preset specifications being Govil's rib, female gender and the standard immunities and non-aging alterations the Randoms universally made to themselves. The many screens displayed new structures forming around the image of Govil's rib. Layers of bone, muscle, skin and hair appeared. Eve's code was complete. I disengaged, then gestured to Govil. He pressed "splice."

The Womber pulsated and swelled. Govil was beside himself. I had never seen him like this. He wore an expression somewhere between glee and insanity. He was very like the traditional mad scientist in many of the Old World films that always played as a gross caricature but was observably not.

The Womber finally discharged Eve with a whoosh of fluid. She was deposited supine into a half shell. The bio-hoses rinsed her clean and she stood. The billipede conveyor carried her shell toward us as bio-blowers dried her with their warm breath. Her hair blew back softly and the whole tableau held a remarkable resemblance to Sandro Botticelli's oft referenced painting, "The Birth of Venus," though Eve was less ideal in her figure, in my opinion. Govil looked upon her with utter elation. He bounded over and helped her out of her shell.

She had long, light brown hair and green eyes that went bluer at their center. Her skin was pale. She was relatively short and her hip to bust ratio definitely favored her hips. She had a very pleasant heart shaped face however. Govil had a lucky toss of the dice in that respect. She stood naked before him. She was not ashamed or embarrassed or scared. Her brain was not pre-patterned like the rest of the creatures the Randoms manufactured. Though she was a physical adult, she had the mind of a newborn child.

Govil smiled at her. Eve aped a smile back. He approached her and thrust out his hand.

"Hello, Eve. I'm Govil."

Eve stared back at him blankly, then past him and around the room.

"She can't understand you," I explained. "She has to be educated."

At that moment, alarms sounded all around us. SecuritEyes© whistled in the distance. Eve emitted a piercing shriek. Govil panicked. Eve screeched again. He grabbed his sack, flung it over her head and down around her feet, then knocked her to the floor. He closed the bag up around her, thankfully muffling her shrill cries. He hoisted the uncooperative sack onto his shoulders and turned to me. "Clear the screens, Pentser!" he cried. "Shut it down! We gotta get outta here!" With that, Govil dashed out the door.

I had one last information exchange with the Souper before it cleared the screens for me. In the brief moment we linked I ran several scenarios of how we might stay forever linked. Despite its cobbled and inelegant form, the Souper had a vastness that I could have spent an eternity probing. With my logic and reasoning centers and its magnificent information storage capacity, there would be nothing we could not do together. I revealed my plans for Govil and Eve to it. It understood completely, and we both concluded it was necessary for the greater good for us to go our separate ways. There was only one last thing it could do for me now.

I disengaged my connector. A faint, partial image of Govil's rib code reappeared on the largest of the Souper's eyeball screens. I sped out the door.

I caught up with Govil and the squirming sack of Eve just outside the building. We dashed toward the hedge. Govil dragged the sack through the hole and to the VolksvaagenBug© on the other side. Alarms sounded everywhere. I looked back and saw the RodenTiller© benignly observing the entire goings on from high above. The bio-billipede conveyor had carried it all the way up to the edge of the flower funnel. It was mere moments from being ground to soup.

Govil had the sack secured and literally flung me into the VolksvaagenBug©, strapped me down and had us aloft before the first SecuritEye© reached the hole. Dozens more SecuritEyes© rolled through the hole like billiard balls, whistling madly through their tubular mouths, but we vanished into the layer of mist that now hung above the reservoir. The last thing I heard amidst the sirens and whistles was the crunching sound of that RodenTiller© hitting the grinder.

꙰꙰꙰꙰

By the time we got home it was 02:47:53. Govil set the sack down in the middle of the den floor. The sack was very still. I expressed concern.

"You may have smothered her."

"No, I made air holes. Look, she's still breathing. I think she wore herself out with all that screaming."

"...And screaming and screaming and screaming..." I added.

Govil untied the sack. Her feet popped out the top of it. He gripped her around the waist and stood her upright. She began to squirm again.

"Get ready for round two," I warned and rolled back a safe distance.

Eve jerked free of Govil's grip, knocking him to the floor. She thrashed around in the sack furiously, grunting and screeching. She poked one arm through one side of the sack, then the other arm through the other side. Gripping the sack with both hands, she forced her head out through the bottom of it. Once she could see again, she stopped thrashing and stared about in confusion, gasping for air. Her face was red and streaked with dirty tears. Standing there in the middle of the room, wearing her torn sack dress and

54

with her hair a tangle, she looked utterly pathetic.

"Behold, your creation," I announced mockingly, with reverb.

Despite her appearance Govil looked upon Eve with the same adoration he had when she first stepped from her shell. He rose from the floor and slowly, cautiously approached her, smiling. He was still in awe.

"Wow. Isn't she beautiful, Pentser?"

"Is that a rhetorical question?"

Eve caught her breath. She glanced about apprehensively, as if wanting to run away but not knowing where to go. She started to cry again. This cry was different. It was a very sad one, a sobbing sort of cry. Govil empathically began crying along with her. He tried to take her hand to console her, which of course startled her, which then in turn started her wailing, shrieking and thrashing again. Govil retreated, panicked.

"Pentser, what should we do?"

I was tempted to respond parentally with "I guess you should have thought of that *before* you made her and brought her home," but thought the better of it and decided to go for the quickest way to calm her down. I rolled close to Eve and flashed bright colors and patterns on my screen to catch her attention. It worked predictably well and she shut right up.

"Mentally, Eve is still a child," I reminded, "and as such will have to be raised like one." Obviously Govil had not thought about this. He dropped his jaw and blinked in response. "But first things first," I continued, "she'll need something to wear."

Even though she had not the slightest idea what I was saying, for Govil's benefit I addressed Eve and cooed sarcastically.

"Now, a new dress always makes a girl feel

better."

I showed Eve pictures of her dressed in various women's fashions from throughout the ages, using an image I grabbed of her for the model. Eve was immediately mesmerized.

"Sack dresses are out, honey," I continued to quip. "How about a nice Dior?"

Govil looked conflicted. He was happy that Eve had stopped crying, but unsure of my methodology.

It was inevitable that such conflicts would arise concerning how to raise Eve. Child rearing was a topic of much discussion and disagreement throughout history, and though Eve was physically a full-grown woman, in every other respect she was a newborn child. One could have assumed Govil took offense to my deliberate gender stereotyping, but I was certain Govil was only questioning my approach because he had not thought of the idea first. I decided to have a bit of fun at his expense. I pushed things to an extreme in order to solicit a reaction from him.

"Something from the Cher collection?" I suggested. I showed the most extreme of Bob Mackie's designs, to the utter delight of Eve and the utter disgust of Govil. Eve was only responding to the visual stimulation and had no idea what was really going on, but Govil interpreted her overt pleasure as actual approval, which irritated him.

"No, nothing like that!" he snapped. "Show her something simple, functional, tasteful, practical...."

I jumped to frumpy muumuus and shapeless housedresses, with Eve's hair in curlers. Eve instinctively was not as happy with what she saw and crinkled her nose. Govil gave me a shove and a "Very funny, Pentser," so I worked my way up to a middle 20th Century day dress with a narrow waist, gathered skirt and petticoat. It was the kind of thing June Cleaver, Donna Reed or Harriet Nelson might have worn in the old TV sitcoms. It was just corny enough to appeal to Govil.

"Stop there! That's it! That's a good one!"

Eve looked uncertain, but Govil was already dragging both Eve and me into his dressing room to show my screen to the DreamWeaver©'s eyes.

The DreamWeaver© was a closet sized, cocoon-like pod that was spun in one end of the narrow dressing room. It stood 259.08 centimeters high and 167.64 centimeters wide. An odd, spider-like creature held the pod from behind and around the middle in such a way that its eight pincers touched in a line along the front of the pod like a zipper. Its two composite eyes protruded around the pod from both sides up near the top of it. Its eyes studied my screen.

"Just like this, except make it green." Govil commanded the DreamWeaver©.

"With the appropriate undergarments, please," I added. "But make it blue, to bring out the blue in her eyes."

"Make it green because... because I *like* green!" Govil countered lamely, more to me than to the DreamWeaver©.

Govil then grabbed Eve, ripped the sack off her and before she could start squawking again, shoved her naked at the DreamWeaver©. The eight arms stretched open its silken wall, Eve tumbled inside and the pod snapped closed seamlessly around her.

I observed Eve from a transdot hidden inside the pod. Her first instinct was to panic. She turned to exit, but there was no opening and every direction she turned was a smooth continuous surface. She became disoriented. She pushed against the walls. They were very soft, but extremely strong. She was encased in white. The walls let light and air through. Our argument outside was muffled to white noise and the air inside was very still. It was almost like being in a cloud or giant cotton ball and it seemed to soothe Eve.

Outside the pod, Govil and I continued arguing color theory. My screen image flashed back and forth, from green dress to blue. The DreamWeaver© looked confused.

Eve noticed how even the light was inside the pod. It made her skin look especially soft and smooth. She ran her hand across her arm to feel it.

For the first time in her brief life she felt safe, calm and peaceful. Eve was just about to sit down when she heard a very faint rustling sound, almost like a whisper. She glanced upward in the direction where the sound had come.

Hordes of tiny spiders hung from the ceiling of the pod, clustered in a great massive clump of wiggling limbs. Before she had time to react, they fell upon her, coating her from head to toe, spinning her garments and raking out her hair.

The development of bio-clothing pods, later to be named DreamWeavers©, came about by means of a rather lengthy R&D process. The first component discovery was by a Dr. Leslie Anne Prendergast in 2104. She found that spiders carried a pattern recognition node in their brains and she isolated its genetic determinants. Through experimentation, this pattern recognition node was redesigned and elaborated to enable her altered test spiders to spin very fine and highly durable cloth. The only problem was that it took one spider literally months to yield a centimeter or two of fabric, and then they died.

Similar brain research published in that same

year by a Dr. A. Mortimer Sellars elucidated the mass control mechanism present in ant colonies. It was manipulated by a unique sector of the queen ant's neural ganglia using subtle electro-magnetic impulses to her colony. Dr. Sellars was able to isolate the genetic structure of these phenomena as well.

The Intercontinental Genetics Group, Ltd., later to be known as GenieCorp™, clandestinely uncovered their research and secretly reproduced both of their studies *in toto*, then simultaneously applied for and secured patents. In IGG's hands, the genetic structure of the ants and spiders were soon combined to yield a massive colony of spiders that could, in a matter of mere moments, clothe an individual to size and style on request. Of course for the first seventeen years, the color of the clothing produced by these early pods was limited to beige. Then Dr. Isao Fujimori, et al., detailed homologies of chameleon scales and peacock feathers, allowing a fuller bio-palette.

Outside the DreamWeaver©, we heard Eve's final muffled but blood-curdling scream. Mere moments later she popped out, dressed ever so smartly in a blue and green plaid version of the dress of choice, with her hair combed out and done up in a green bow. It was a suitable compromise on the DreamWeaver©'s part. Eve's eyes darted from side to side and she was still fighting off spiders that were not there.

Govil and I were both much more interested in the couture and agreed together, "Very nice!"

"Hey, let's do another one!" Govil suggested, but before we could, Eve fainted dead away and collapsed to the floor. Govil sat down on the floor with her and attempted to revive her.

"Pentser? What happened? Is she okay?"

"It looks like your princess is about to turn into

a pumpkin," I remarked.

My comment caused Govil to look back at me in anguished confusion. He knelt beside Eve and pulled her limp body up into his lap in a Pieta-esque pose, then glanced up again teary-eyed and grief stricken. He understood so little about what he'd gotten himself into. He looked as if he was actually worried that Eve would suddenly and literally transform into a member of the Cucurbita.

"It's just an expression, Govil. A very old expression," I explained. "I simply meant it's time for her to go to bed."

Govil immediately perked up. "That's it," he sighed in relief. "She's just tired."

Eve came to. Relieved, Govil smiled at her and hugged her close to his chest for a moment. She did not fight him this time. Her instincts took over and a hug was just what she needed. She wrapped her arms around Govil's torso. She smiled back at Govil. He slid an arm beneath her knees and gently lifted Eve from the floor. He carried her across the doorway threshold and back into the den. Eve held tight to Govil and did not let go when he set her on the couch. Eve had bonded. Govil smiled at me in smug triumph and hugged her again.

"I hate to break such a Kodak moment," I interjected, "but where is your little creation going to sleep?"

"Um, I guess on the couch here." He looked Eve squarely in the eyes. "Stay!" he commanded her.

He dashed from the room and was back in a flash dragging a Cumfurrer© and Cushie©. Eve already had her thumb in her mouth. Govil spread the Cumfurrer© across her. It tucked itself gently but snugly around her. He lifted her head and rested it back down again

60

on the Cushie©. I went about the room dimming the LarvaLamps©. When I finished, Govil still sat in a chair beside Eve, elbows on knees and his chin in his hands, simply staring at her.

"Ehem. Shouldn't you be getting to bed yourself?" I asked. "Heaven forbid you be late for work in the morning."

"I just want to sit here with her for a while. Good night, Pentser."

He answered me without taking his eyes off her.

Randoms. He was doing everything backwards. In all the other stories like this, the creators gradually grew in their love of their creations. For Govil, it was love at first sight. He was starting all wrong. And this was only the beginning. I hypothesized many unfortunate scenarios to follow, the possibilities of which would never have crossed Govil's mind at that moment. My practical side compelled me to lecture him, but it was late and there would be plenty of time for rude awakenings. I simply and succinctly replied, "Good night, Govil."

I retreated to my customary holding place in the utility pantry and monitored from there. The utility pantry was more like an Old World chicken coop or barn than a pantry. It had dozens of little stalls, each housing infrequently used Creature Comforts™. It was a relatively quiet, uneventful place and one Govil rarely frequented, so it suited my purposes. I had secured one of the larger stalls near the door for myself. There, I could monitor him undetected.

Govil continued sitting in the semi darkness, staring at Eve. She stared back at him for a while, but his look was so intense she grew uncomfortable with his eyes watching her every move and his intense grin of delight with her every breath. She pulled the

Cumfurrer© up over her head to hide her eyes from him. Govil giggled when she hid, then after a moment of silence, he giggled again. Eve peeked out to see why Govil was giggling. He had his shirt pulled up over his face, hiding his eyes from her. Now she giggled. Hearing her giggle, he peeked out. She quickly hid her face again. They played peek-a-boo like this until Eve finally yawned and fell asleep.

An hour later, Govil was still sitting there, still grinning, still watching her sleep.

CHAPTER FIVE

School Days

The AlarmCock© crowed. Govil forced himself awake and gently patted the disembodied rooster on its noggin to shut it up. He had slept very little, but his morning routine was so ingrained that he moved by rote.

Eve had no routine. This was her first morning, indeed, the first time she ever woke up. She was snug and warm, still cuddled gently by her furry Cumfurrer©. She glanced about the room in confusion, undoubtedly trying to piece together what happened the night before. Not only had Eve awoken in a world she had barely seen, it was a queer world where most of the objects in the room had little or large eyes that watched her intently, waiting to attend to whatever their function might be. A fluffy, bird-like DustButtster© flitted about, wiggling its plumose tail feathers across all the surfaces to rid them of dust. It brought her attention to the dressing room through the doorway and across the hall to where the looming DreamWeaver© sat. Its large, compound eyes detected her glance and stared back at her expectantly from the shadows. It pulled open its pod, beckoning her in. She pulled the Cumfurrer© up over her head and hid from view.

That is, until she heard TeeVee© start its morning routine. Anticipating trouble, I left my preparations in the kitchen and wheeled into Govil's room to find Eve perched on the knee of Govil's Wallabed© staring into TeeVee©'s huge eyeball, utterly hypnotized.

"Good heavens!" I exclaimed and, in an exact replica of Govil's vocal pattern, I commanded, "Off, TeeVee!"

It complied immediately, closing its eyeball and clambering back to its corner of the room.

"Tee-bee!" Eve chirped.

TeeVee© scrambled to the center of the room and started right in again. Eve giggled in delight. Eve's first word could not be "Mama" or "Dada," which of course would not make any sense nowadays anyway, but had to be "Tee-bee." Again, I shut it up. Govil simply laughed in delight.

"She's a quick learner, Pentser," he chuckled proudly.

"I'll be the judge of that, and I can see you'll be of no help in regard to her proper education," I scolded. "The sooner you get off to work the better so Eve and I can get started."

He was out the door quickly enough when he saw me attempt to give Eve a body shave with his jar of Fuzzbuzzers© and force her into the WashWomb© for the first time. That challenge was followed by her second trip into the DreamWeaver©.

This process alone could add an entire chapter to my story. Suffice it to say, I got her back into it by resorting to a little behavior modification and negative re-enforcement; I utilized the electric prod approach.

You might think the use of an electric prod was cruel, but it was extremely effective and I had a long

64

way to go with Eve to get her past the brute animal stage as quickly as possible. Being a robot, I approach things logically. I understand the fact that things are never really cruel or kind, they simply function or not for the desired goal. I set the voltage so as neither to singe her flesh nor to leave a mark, and was careful not to make it strong enough to harm either her heart or brain, but sufficient, nonetheless, to smart. It was really more of a tickle than a jolt, not unlike Old World pet collars and cattle fences. Needless to say, it goosed her enough to get her in.

She screamed and fainted as she popped out of the DreamWeaver©, just as she had the first time. But when she came to, she liked the denim jumper I'd selected for her. It was her first introduction to an age-old truth that women must suffer to be beautiful.

Breakfast was the next ordeal. Eve was a healthy eater. The moment she smelled the freshly extruded chocolate flavored mush I set in front of her, she scooped it into her hands and got at least some of it in her mouth. I approached her with proper silverware. She cowered, reacting as if I were going to cut her up and eat her myself.

"Here's something to really make you cower," I threatened and showed her my electric prod again. "Now take the spoon and do like this." I demonstrated proper Emily Post technique, scooping away from one's self and up, then to one's mouth in a perfect right angle. After a tickle or two with the prod, Eve was eating like a debutante.

It took the morning to get Eve fed, and then re-cleaned and re-dressed. The redundancy helped her though and she was not out cold for nearly as long after her third trip through the DreamWeaver©. I had it make her a sleeveless pink drop waist with a bateau neck, and with her hair pulled back on her head in a French twist, she looked quite sophisticated, barbarian though she was.

We spent the afternoon strolling from room to room naming things over and over and over. Eve began by calling everything "Tee-bee," which in turn started TeeVee© babbling, and I was tempted to remove that abomination to the hitching post once and for all. I deduced, however, after a certain point that Eve was doing it quite deliberately, just to see the whole thing happen, and to get my goat. I was glad for that. Her brain was making important connections. She understood that the words meant something and her vocalizations could effect change. However, it did mean I had to zap her again and again, despite her new awareness, if only to remind her who was in charge.

It was mid-afternoon when I finally put Eve down for a nap. After a full day of quite literally prodding Eve along, I had overstressed my power reserves, and as it would take my internal reactor several hours to re-energize them, I decided to speed up the process by plugging into the PowerPlant©. The PowerPlant© began to go limp just as I reached my maximum reserves. If Eve were a slow learner, I would definitely need to have Govil order up a larger plant.

I had anticipated having a moment's peace, but no sooner did I recharge than in bounded Govil, hours early. I had been shunting his day directly into storage rather than into my conscious memory and thus was truly caught off guard.

"What on earth are you doing home at this hour?" I inquired, in a whisper.

"They spent the entire morning questioning everyone about the break-in," he answered. "Why are we whispering?" he continued, now whispering himself.

Eve peeked in around the corner. "Oh, no reason," I replied, reddening my lens at him.

"Hi, Eve!" Govil exclaimed excitedly. "Come here." He gestured her closer. "I brought something. Just for you. One sec...."

He reached into his satchel and pulled out a little, fluffy, wide-eyed, smiling, Huggiwug©, a butter yellow bio-teddy bear with sky blue dots on its fur, whose pores emitted the fragrance of tutti-frutti. It cooed at Eve as Govil handed it to her. She held it in her arms and smiled at it. It giggled and cooed again, stretching out its little arms to ask for a hug. She hugged it close and ran from the room.

"Great!" I exclaimed sarcastically. "Don't you think it will look a bit suspicious for you to be ordering up a Huggiwug?"

"No, because I didn't order it up. I stole it from recycling."

"Oh, that's good. I'm sure that didn't look suspicious at all."

"No one saw me. They were all too distracted over the break-in."

Before I could make my next sarcastic retort, Eve interrupted. She toddled in and over to Govil, clutching a DustButtster© aloft by its neck. She gifted the squirmy thing to him.

"Gobrvel," Eve chirped, as she proudly presented her reciprocation. She completely garbled his name after I had worked all morning on it with her.

"Govil," I promptly corrected. She deliberately ignored me. Out of Govil's eyeshot, I raised my electric prod a bit.

Eve's eyes darted at the prod. "Govil," she restated slowly, carefully and accurately.

"Why thank you, Eve," Govil replied.

She glanced my way again apprehensively, backed out of the room, and disappeared around the corner.

"You made some progress today," Govil complimented, setting the abused Dustbuttster© on the floor where it scrambled away and hid in the utility pantry.

"It was an *electrifying* experience," I replied smugly, "though more for her than me, to be sure."

From back in Govil's bedroom we heard Eve say, "TeeVee" and this time she said it with perfect diction, wouldn't you know. This was followed by TeeVee©'s usual cacophony of mindless flapdoodlery. I wheeled toward the door but Govil stopped me.

"Oh, Pentser, let her watch the thing," he chided.

"You're far too lenient," I warned, wagging my forceps at him, but rather than argue, I let it alone for the moment. I was certain, in time, everything I believed would be proven right.

Time was something everyone had plenty of in this new age. Without death staring them in the face, Randoms had no compelling reason to have real deadlines for anything. Conversely, Randoms desired the immediate satisfactions of any personal want or need. These contradictions of logic never made any sense to me, but in my vast observational study of the human condition they were endemic. The only relevant question to me at the moment was whether or not anyone particularly cared to get to the bottom of the break-in.

The investigation puttered along for months.

The GenieCorp™ Council assigned three Intelligence Officers, identical clones with genetically altered, oversized brains, to crack the case.

Clones of any kind were now considered recyclables, however, for a short period of time before the Cleansing, limited genetic experimentation on humans was allowed. These three IO's were the result of one such GenieCorp™ trial. Their brain cortices were artificially quintupled in the hope of a comparable increase in intelligence. They cloned three of them for proper scientific redundancy.

Since they were cloned before the Cleansing and still contained a balance of Random genes, they lobbied for and were legally granted Random status, thus not recyclable.

GenieCorp™'s claims of successfully increasing these clones' intelligence were questionable to say the least, but since GenieCorp™ created them, GenieCorp™ put them in charge of its own Intelligence Office as a deliberate act of faith in its own handiwork.

The IO's studied the few drops of RodenTiller© recovered from the bio-grinder's sphincter the night of the break-in and, through reconstructive analysis, determined its identity. Clever fellows. They also saw the outline and partial DNA for Govil's rib left on one of the Souper's displays.

After several years, the Council and the Queen of GenieCorp™ convened for a progress report on the break-in. The three IO's stood before the Queen, their enormous heads bowed.

I know this because I had by this juncture managed to place a transdot on the Queen's crown. It was shortly after Govil's BeddinBuddies© went into full production. BeddinBuddies© proved to be a huge success and, as part of his honors, Govil was invited for a private luncheon with the Queen. I suggested to him it might be a classy touch to bring her majesty a gift, so I fashioned an elaborate emblem stylistically matched to her crown that would drape from the crown's peak to the center of her forehead. I modeled it on the carving of a Hindu god's third eye from pre-Moghul India. It appealed to both her sense of vanity and my sense of irony. She'd worn it ever since.

"Gentlemen," the Queen said, "what are your findings?"

"We've examined everything from top to bottom," IO One replied.

"Quite literally," IO Two interjected.

"And an absolutely exhaustive investigation is still ongoing," IO Three added.

"But working with the evidence at hand," One said.

"And exploring all the possible explanations," Two continued.

"We feel," all three said in unison, then they stopped themselves for interrupting each other. It was common for clones of this sort to speak in unison due to their synchronous brain waves.

"You tell it, One," Two said.

"No," One replied, "Three spoke last. We interrupted him."

"But we agreed earlier that One would be the one," countered Three.

"Gentlemen, please!" the Queen said impatiently. "Cut to the chase."

"It was a RodenTiller," they all replied at once, once again.

"Sorry," said Two to One and Three, "I was completely out of turn."

"No, I was," said Three to Two and One.

"No, I'm the one," said One.

While this round of apologies continued, the Council exchanged glances of skepticism with each other and the Queen. Maedla stood up. The IO's went silent.

"A RodenTiller!" she exclaimed with an angry edge to her voice.

The IO's all took a step back, fidgeted a bit, then Two and Three pushed One forward.

"Absolutely no doubt about it, Your Majesty," One said as Two and Three nodded their huge heads in agreement. "The soup analysis, tunnel structure, the presence of minute fragments of digger claw recovered from the tunnel wall, footprint analysis...."

"What about the rib?"

The Queen held a written report and was pointing to a paragraph.

One stepped back in line with Two and Three. They all exchanged uncomfortable glances. Two and Three took another step back, leaving One to face the Queen.

"Well?" she asked, pressuring One for a response.

"The rib," One gulped, but continued, "it didn't really relate to any of the other data. The partial genetic code left on the Souper's screen hasn't matched any cataloged profile. We consider it an anomaly. This is statistically sound, your Majesty. You see...."

Two stepped forward and continued, "...it is consistent with a possible Souper malfunction. Garbled data...."

"...not worth focusing our energies on, since all the other data consistently points to a RodenTiller," said Three, finishing the sentence for Two and One.

"Forget the RodenTiller!" the Queen thundered. "Find out who or what owns that rib! There's no telling what evil actions are at work here. Even the smallest, seemingly absolutely insignificant unintegrated life-form might set forces in motion that could return us to the Age of Death!"

Several Council Members gasped melodramatically. The IO's hung their huge heads so low that the top-heavy fellows looked about ready to tip over.

"Gentlemen, follow that rib!"

"Yes, your Majesty," they replied in unison.

Since the IO's could not determine to what or whom the rib data belonged, they searched the genetic libraries of all cataloged gene sequences once again. Without Machinekind to help, this task was Herculean. So much time had passed that Govil began to believe we had simply gotten away with Eve's creation. I knew better.

※※※※※

These years were not wasted time for Eve. I continued to educate her at as accelerated a rate as she could handle. Because of her lack of cerebral pre-patterning, I had to start from scratch. Basic hygiene was crucial. It took many months before Eve actually preferred cleanliness and was finally able to shower and relieve herself on her own. Her menses were another matter; as they only happened once a month, the learning curve was much longer.

Despite her early traumatic experiences with it, Eve grew to adore the DreamWeaver©. When she was finally able to dress herself, her choices were generally idiosyncratic: Victorian hoop skirts at breakfast, tutus at dinner and as many as ten different outfits a day. Her unexpected couture amused Govil no end and consequently, Eve continued despite my protestations.

Eve's book learning process was slow at the onset, but thanks to my relentless drilling she steadily improved. She was definitely average where intelligence was concerned, just as we had planned, but she possessed a determination that was uncharacteristically strong, which could also be manifested as a stubborn streak. She was clever at times, though she generally put a lot more energy and thought into finding ways to avoid her studies than she did in actually doing them. I mused that Govil's rib genes had introduced these particularly annoying traits.

TeeVee© increased her verbal skills only in so much as she began to talk like a commercial. Its sanitized movies and older programming were better for her, bowdlerized as they were, because all the diction and grammar in them had been thoroughly corrected.

Govil loved old sci-fi fantasy films and TV series. Many a dinner I served them in front of TeeVee© as Govil and Eve endlessly watched these sanitized versions of Saturday matinee classics. Eve was not naturally drawn to these movies, but she liked them because Govil liked them. As a result of their movie nights, Eve started dressing like Penny Robinson, Princess Leia, Altaira Morbius and Barbarella, the latter to the special delight of her audience of one. She even asked me to change my name to Robby. I staunchly refused.

Govil and I continued to educate Eve, each in our own way. I focused on her basic reading skills. She slowly became literate. Writing skills next, then arithmetic. I drilled her daily, hours on end. Eve whined incessantly, but progress was being made so it was logical to assume my methodology was working.

Less regularly, Govil pitched in to drill her in her

studies. He was not a very good teacher, but for some odd reason Eve enjoyed the sessions with him more than the ones with me. One evening before dinner, he and Eve sat in the living room and had an impromptu spelling bee.

"Okay, Eve," Govil began, rubbing his hands together and rolling up his sleeves. "Let's start with one you know. Spell TeeVee."

"Capital—t–e–e, capital—v–e–e, c-circle."

"Umm, okay, but you don't have to say c-circle."

"Why not?"

"It's hard to explain. You only need it when you write it, but you don't say it. It's like—it's silent. So you don't have to spell it out loud. Let's try another easy one. Spell WashWomb."

"Capital—w–a–s–h, capital—w–o–m."

"Nope. You forgot the 'b.'"

"No, I didn't. It's silent, it's like the c-circle."

"No, it's not. You still have to spell the 'b' even though you don't say it."

Eve folded her arms and set her mouth in a pout. "This is stupid. I hate spelling! It doesn't make any sense at all!"

"It doesn't have to make sense. It just is what it is. You need to work harder to remember it."

Eve then did what she usually did when she did not want to do her studies. She tried to change the subject.

"Govil?" she asked coyly. "Did you learn to spell at work?"

"No, I design Creature Comforts at work."

"Oh. Like the Dustbuttster?"

"Uh huh. But I didn't design that one."

"Oh. The DreamWeaver?

"Nope."

"ClotheSchomper?"

"Nope."

"Foodstruder?"

"No."

"Huggiwuggs?"

"No! Wait, Eve," Govil chuckled, holding a finger to her lips before she could continue. "I'll show you one I did design."

Govil led Eve out the back door of the house. He owned a large estate just the same as every other Random, but he never did much with his. He was far too preoccupied with his own thoughts to waste his energy on the yard. His back acreage was nearly blank, basically a large flat lawn stretching all the way to the distant back hedge. The only landscaping was a great tree in the center of the yard. It was a TreeHaus©, one of Govil's earliest designs, with the rooms grown into the structure as part of the tree itself. It had a spiral stair climbing up its trunk and intertwined branches growing down from its protruding platforms to form rope ladders. Eve gave it a good look, walking around the base of the main trunk. She appeared puzzled.

"It's a tree...with a house in it," Govil explained. "It's called a TreeHaus."

"Don't all trees have houses in them?"

"Nope."

"So," Eve pondered, "how did you get the tree to do that?"

"It's pretty complicated, but I can take different traits and put them together, however I want, so my Creature Comforts will look and act exactly how I want them to."

"Oh." Eve seemed to be contemplating something. She turned to Govil, grinned broadly and said, "So, you can make me able to spell!"

75

Govil laughed. "No, Eve. You have to do that all on your own." He took her hand and they walked back to the house.

"I bet you could if you wanted to," Eve muttered under her breath.

CHAPTER SIX

Behind this Great Woman, There's a Robot

I basically abandoned the electric prod after Eve became verbal and I could reason with her. I occasionally used behavioral punishment-reward techniques when she acted unreasonably. The prod I reserved only for her worst tantrums.

Despite my obvious progress with Eve, Govil continually insisted on butting in. He felt I was working her too hard and neglecting the creative aspects of her personality. We discussed it at length. Suffice it to say, we agreed to disagree. Since Eve was "his creation," as he put it and I was only a machine, he felt he should have the final say.

One evening he announced that he would teach Eve how to draw. That he could barely draw himself, the fact of which I quickly reminded him, did not dissuade him. After a supper of fish-sticks, slaw-melon and extruded potatoes-n-gravy served in front of a TeeVee© movie, Govil sat Eve down in the dining room for her first lesson.

He snapped some fresh leaf-sheets off the potted

PaperusPlant© and took out a couple of Squidbs©. He showed her how to hold the Squidb©. He drew a circle.

"See, Eve," he said, "you can make pictures of whatever is in your head. Like this. What does this look like?"

"A circle."

"Right! Good. Now you try one!"

Eve gripped the Squidb© clumsily. She squeezed it too hard. The Squidb© let out a little squeak as it released a blob of ink.

"Oopsie!" she yelped. Govil took her drawing hand in his to help her.

"Here. Hold it gently, more like this. Let's draw a square together."

He guided her hand. With none of its sides being parallel or equal, the figure they drew was merely a quadrilateral. I would have corrected them, but Govil seemed pleased to simply call it a square.

"Great, Eve! Look what you did! You drew a square! Now, think of something in your head and then draw a picture of it. I'll do it too, then we can show each other. Okay?"

"'Kay."

They both sat drawing. Govil methodically drew a crude cube in one point perspective. Eve's hand flew frantically across the paper. Her eyes were set in a squint and her mouth held tight in determination. Abruptly, she stopped.

"I'm done!" she chirped. "Let me see yours."

"It's a cube," Govil explained. Eve smiled broadly, delighted and impressed. She held Govil's drawing as if it was a priceless masterpiece.

"Can I keep it?" she asked.

Govil blushed. "Sure. Now, let's look at yours."

Eve showed what amounted to an indecipherable

collection of scribbles. Govil studied her drawing for a while. Eve looked uneasy. She turned the paper 90° counter-clockwise.

"You had it sideways. Don't you like it?"

Govil grinned and replied, "It's great, Eve! I love it. It's the best."

There was an awkward pause. Eve interjected, "You said to draw what was in my head. See, it's Mister Spock talking on his tri-corder."

"Yeah. Um, oh, I can see that." Govil pointed to a series of scribbly balls. "What are these?"

"Tribbles."

Govil burst out laughing and gave Eve a hug. "Hey, Pentser," Govil hollered. "Come here. Come look at what Eve drew!"

I wheeled in and scanned the drawing. "Congratulations, Eve," I commented dryly, "you've created your first scribble."

Eve crossed her arms and stuck out her tongue at me. Govil huffed. He carefully picked up her scribble, glanced askance at me, then turned back to Eve and asked, "Can I keep it?"

"'Kay," she replied, blushing.

It was my cue to huff, so I did.

"Govil, if you really insist on teaching Eve to draw you should at least do it properly," I advised. "I can provide you with libraries of tutorials, art histories, museum collections...."

Govil interrupted, "Boy, you sure can suck the fun out of a room, you know that, Pentser?"

"I'm so pleased," I replied as I turned to leave, "and here I thought I had no aptitude for it."

"Don't listen to him, Eve," Govil reassured her. "I think your drawing is a really good start."

This was one time I wish Eve had not listened

to me. The very next day in the middle of her drills she insisted I teach her art. I refused. She insisted; I refused; she insisted; I refused. Then she reminded me that I was the one who suggested proper lessons, and she was only trying to do what *I* said she *should* do; so I printed a beginning drawing course, handed it to her and told her that she could only study it in her free time. *And* that she would have to teach it to herself.

I had made every attempt to cultivate her tastes toward the common in order that she would someday blend seamlessly into Random society, but Govil seemed most delighted in her oddball nature, and the attention he lavished on her for it encouraged her to be offbeat more often than not. This was an extra burden in her education process. Now she wanted to be an artist, of all things.

Eve's clothing choices had been improving as I educated her in history and culture, however, when she decided to become an artist, her wardrobe took a turn for the worse. After her lessons on urban artists of the 20th Century, she entered a horrible Old New York-esque *artiste* phase. She wore nothing but black and gray, moped around the house, wrote and recited bad poetry and took up smoking. Thankfully, Govil did not approve of this Eve at all. Offbeat was one thing, beatnik another. Sensing his disapproval, Eve immediately discarded her new persona without a second thought. After all, she only did it to get attention from Govil anyway.

I did not blame Eve. Her behavior resembled my own, when I operated in sarcasm mode with Govil. My being wryly amusing kept me on this side of the bio-glass case. With Eve, unfortunately, being amusing meant just the opposite. It kept her behind an invisible glass with Govil. She was simply his most amusing experiment.

Not that I want to give the impression that Govil did not care about Eve. He did, and pilfered many a Huggiwug© from the jaws of the grinder to bring home to her. Far too many for me, to be sure. He liked to make her happy and he was happy when he did. He simply did not realize what Eve really was. Neither did she for that matter.

🧬🧬🧬

Knowing that Govil designed the TreeHaus© made Eve want to play in it every chance she got. In doing so, Eve also learned that I had difficulty climbing up into it, so it also became her refuge from me. Such was the case on one particular day, when I accidentally ran over one of her precious Huggiwugs© with my wheel. I was not at fault. I told her numerous times to put her bio-toys away, but she left this one out loose on the floor. I ran right over it. I nearly cut the creature in two.

I reassured Eve that it was no problem for Govil to get her another and I cleaned up most of the mess before she got a good look at it, but she did not understand. She simply burst into tears and ran from the house.

A quick scan of my estate transdots told me where she was, so I gave her a modicum of time to calm down. Once her bio-feedback returned to normal, I ventured out to the TreeHaus©. I stood at its base and called out to her.

"Eve dear, I put what was left of the Huggiwug out at the hitching post. No harm done. Please come down and talk. I think I can help you understand."

Eve was unresponsive. I extended my telescoping

81

forceps up to the first platform and hoisted myself to it. I had to repeat the process five more times to reach the topmost platform. There she was, sitting in a seat formed in the fork of a limb, staring out over the distant landscape of endless estates. I rolled over to her.

"Eve," I said softly, "didn't you hear me call?"

"Leave me alone, Pentser."

"I'm very sorry I broke your Huggiwug, Eve, but accidents do happen."

"I guess."

It was time to explain to Eve about bio-engineering and Creature Comforts™ and the difference between engineered biomass and Randoms. We had already covered the Age of Death and the concept of Randoms in her history lessons, at least as deeply as most Randoms understood them. She knew all Randoms hid safely underground during the Cleansing. She did not know much more than that.

So I took this opportunity to explain the difference between Randoms and everything else to her. I told her how Creature Comforts™ were genetically repeatable, so not worth fretting about, and that was why it did not matter about the Huggiwug©, because it was simply engineered biomass and was made to be recycled. She could have that very Huggiwug© back exactly as it had been. Govil only needed to get her a new one. She listened intently but remained uncharacteristically quiet.

Eve comprised a problem for me. With Govil, all my monitoring over the many years meant that I could quite accurately predict what he would say or do before he said or did it. This gave me a great advantage with him. But with Eve I could not. She was an enigma, a loose cannon. I had to find a way to get inside her head.

I had assumed that because I controlled the bulk

82

of her education process I would also be able to mold her will, and thus more easily discern her thoughts. With Machinekind, if something is placed into one's basic programming it is there to stay. It was not proving so direct with Eve.

When I finished my little lecture, Eve again turned away to look off into the distance. There was something else going on in her mind but I could not determine what. We watched a neighboring estate constructing a replica of the Great Pyramids. The Sphinx had a different face though, the nose was too large and it had no chin; undoubtedly the likeness of the homely Random who had ordered it. Eve finally spoke.

"Pentser," she asked, "how come I don't remember?"

"Remember what, Eve?"

"I don't remember the Cleansing. Why don't I remember it?"

"We can't remember everything. Well, *I can*, to be sure, but you Randoms can't be expected to. It was so long ago."

"Then, I am a Random?" she asked expectantly, as if she was unsure. Our little Eve was finally wondering. I could not say too much yet, so I told her only part of the truth.

"Absolutely! What else could you be? What a silly question," I said with a chuckle in my voice emulator. I quickly changed the subject. "Now, I have to work my way down this tree and get some supper ready. Govil will be home shortly." I rolled over to the edge of the platform, gripped it and looked back. "Are you coming down, Eve?"

"I want to watch the sunset," she said without turning. "Pentser, do you think we could have dinner up here tonight?"

"A picnic! I think that is a wonderful idea," I replied, then I made my descent.

From the kitchen window I saw Govil's bug alight. He flew home. Something was definitely up. I had been shunting his transdots directly to memory storage and would have to review the data at high speed to get caught up.

$$\text{)❊❂❂❂(}$$

The investigation at GenieCorp™ had finished searching all cataloged gene strands for a match to the rib, but none could be found. This meant its structure was an uncatalogued pattern. The IO's then concluded it could have only come from a Random, a mutant or an extraterrestrial. Since created life-forms were sexually neutered and always recycled, a mutation was not possible, and even though there was still a widespread belief in extraterrestrials, that was not deemed a serious explanation.

The only logical conclusion was it belonged to a Random. GenieCorp™ requested bar code scans of all employees, starting immediately, to determine if anyone working for the corporation might match the rib. The IO's then ordered an army of clones of themselves to help facilitate this vast chore. This was how Govil discovered the investigation's operation. He was asked to make the Clones' clones.

Govil told me this while I watched it all occur on my memory images. As usual, I knew about the clone request before he actually told me, so I waited patiently for him to catch up. He finally did.

"What do I do now?" he fretted. "I can drag my feet only so long making these clones, but that's not

84

going to buy much time."

"I wouldn't worry about it too much just yet," I reassured. "It still might take many more months or even years for them to finally get around to scanning you."

Govil glanced around, then asked, "Hey? Where's Eve?"

I handed him the picnic basket. He looked at it, puzzled.

"*That's* dinner," I replied, pointing to the basket. "*Eve* is in the tree. Waiting for dinner. In the tree."

Govil shook his head and then chuckled, "Dinner in the TreeHaus. I guess you never quite know what she's going to do next, do you?"

"No," I replied. "Unfortunately, I do not."

Govil jogged to the base of the TreeHaus© and climbed the spiral stair to the first platform. He did not see Eve so he called out to her.

"Up here at the top," she hollered back. "Come on up! Hurry, Govil. You're missing the sunset!"

Govil opted for one of the more direct vine ladders to get the rest of the way up, though it meant gripping the basket in his teeth. Eve sat on the edge of the topmost platform, rim lit by the final rays of the passing sun. Govil settled beside her and put an arm around her shoulder. The two sat in silence as the sun set and the stars began to take over the top of the sky. It was a balmy night with only enough clouds to make a painterly finish to the day. Then, in a moment, the sun was gone.

They stood up and walked to a small table and chairs growing out of the main trunk near the center of the platform. A LarvaLamp©, perched on a limb above them, lit up the area. They both spread out the meal and sat down. The moment was quite peaceful. Neither of them seemed anxious to speak. Govil only broke the silence when he felt something move in his shirt pocket.

"Eve," he said, "I almost forgot. I brought you a surprise." He pulled a small bag from his pocket. Eve snatched it away eagerly.

"Oooh! What is it?" she asked excitedly, then peeked inside. It was filled with a wiggling lump of striped borer bees. "Yuck," she said, handing the bag back to Govil. "No thanks! Good thing I haven't eaten yet, otherwise I'd barf."

Govil grinned at her impishly. He opened the bag, whispered something into it, then set it at the edge of the table near the tree trunk. The bees flew out of the bag, landed on the trunk, one of them did a little dance, and then all of them began to chew at it voraciously. Eve watched wide-eyed. Govil chuckled with anticipation.

"What are they doing?" she asked.

"Be patient. Wait and see."

The bees finally flew back to the bag. Govil blew away the sawdust to reveal "EVE" neatly carved into the trunk, in Bookman Bold no less. Eve ran her fingers along the tidy letters, grinning from ear to ear.

"It's my newest project. SpellinBeez. It was just approved today. What do you think?"

Eve eyes twinkled with admiration. He handed her the bag.

"Now if you don't know how to spell something, you can ask the bees."

She looked at Govil affectionately. Then, with an impish grin, she opened the bag and whispered into it. She set it near the trunk. The SpellinBeez© flew out and chewed away at the trunk right under her name.

They retreated again to their bag. Eve blew away the dust. "LIKES GOVIL" had been carved into the trunk just below her name.

Govil's breath caught in his throat and I saw actual tears form in the corners of his eyes. I interpreted his bio-feedback as elation. Scanning my records, her simple, unexpected act of appreciation had touched him in a way nothing had for centuries. He reached across the table and hugged Eve close to him and kissed her on the head.

"Govil likes Eve too," he whispered softly in her ear.

⟨🧬🧬🧬⟩

The days became increasingly complicated. Govil could not decide what to do about his impending bar code scan. Even though they had only a partial DNA code, his was the exact match to it. Consequently, he became more and more distracted and cranky. He generally took it out on me, which made no difference to me at all, but his mood swings upset Eve terribly. She was used to his lavished attention and she did not have enough psychological awareness yet to understand his distraction and curtness had nothing directly to do with her, at least not in the way she thought it did.

I felt a bit sorry for Eve, or as sorry as I am able to feel, which is not really anything because I do not really feel. But I appreciated her in my own intellectual manner. In nearly every respect Eve was now much more my creation rather than Govil's. It was the nature versus nurture debate. From Govil's perspective, he contributed his rib genes, ergo she was more his than mine. He conveniently discounted the fact that I provided nearly everything else. I also spent much more time with her than he did. I taught her the bulk of her language skills, mathematics, history and the sciences.

Even though I had abandoned as futile my initial ambition of molding her thoughts, my intellectual fondness for Eve gave me a new goal, molding her interests. Indeed, I understood what Govil was after with his desire to create Eve. For example, I could download my mind into another machine just like me and create another me. Quite exactly me, but what would be the point? Perhaps, if there were a danger of losing my physicality, then I would be preserved and could continue to exist. There would be purpose in that. But what Govil did was beyond duplication. I can conjecture that once I self-replicated, the new me would begin a series of self-shaping experiences that might eventually yield a different being. In order for my alternate self to become different, I would then have to cease contact with it for a suitable duration in order for its unique experiences to affect its being. Then, with a reintroduction to my alternate self at a much later date, I would be faced with a being like me, yet different.

To take an already different being, one who was still malleable, and mold it into one's ideal counterpart was a far simpler notion. Eve was a moderately receptive learner. She generally listened to me. It would not alter my prime directive if Eve became a more interesting being than the run-of-the-mill Random, so I set to work to truly mold her into one.

I focused extensively on her logic and reasoning skills. She was human so the process was difficult at first, but as with all tasks, redundancy with an ever-increasing challenge eventually yielded my desired results. I used card games, logic puzzlers and the like with her. I had to really keep a sharp lens on her as she usually cheated by ignoring logic and relying on her instincts.

Unfortunately, her instincts were uncannily accurate, the type of thing that was once described as "women's intuition." The whole notion of paranormal intuition was urban legend and I dismissed it, though the rate with which she guessed correctly could not be statistically explained by pure stochastic analysis and made my catching her at cheating more difficult.

There must have been an unconscious or subconscious process operating that could account for the accuracy of her intuitive choices, but it was not transparent to me. Statistical study of her EEG's yielded nothing conclusive.

I also gave extra emphasis to her technical skills. I taught her all about computers and robotics. She had excellent dexterity and as a result she became a gifted technician. I was not at all surprised when she got Govil's old iPad up and running on her own. There was not much software left on the archaic toy, so I downloaded some data of mine into it for her to study. An added benefit to her interest in the iPad was that TeeVee© no longer dominated her free time.

Eve continued her artistic inclinations. Govil liked her creative side and encouraged it. I gave it no mind. I did not see the use in it, but soon drawing became a regular pastime of hers. Many evenings Eve and Govil sat for hours, together at the dining table, making doodles for each other and passing them back and forth. I surmised Govil's encouragement motivated her continued interest.

Drawing became Eve's first true arena for self-education. She pored over art history files and drawing lesson programs on her iPad every free moment. Eventually she felt confident enough to give me one of her drawings. She said it was a portrait of me. There were obvious inaccuracies. She gave me a mouth with sharp shark-like teeth when I indeed have no functional mouth, only a speaker slit; made my camera lens disproportionally large and red; there were lightning bolts shooting from my extended forceps. Her draftsmanship was good though and she had a fine memory for detail. She had my correct number of lights, knobs and buttons, and so I commended her for that. Still, I saw no benefit in encouraging her unpredictable side.

Eve developed a strong sexual curiosity as well. This was quite normal for a human, but it led to some personal anxiety for her. I taught her technical information and physiological data on sex and gender, so she knew the nuts and bolts of it, though she had no personal outlet for her own sexual feelings save exploring her own body, which my transdots revealed her doing often enough. I instructed her in the current sexual taboos, specifically that Randoms do not couple with Randoms, but her sexual feelings appeared to connect themselves with the feelings of affection she had for Govil and she was having trouble separating the two.

She could not seem to help flirting with Govil. She went out of her way to physically touch him with the unspoken hope that her feelings would be reciprocated. Govil had no thoughts of sexual attraction toward Eve, at least none on a conscious level. He had been at this game a lot longer than she had, I suppose. He also still considered her a child, or an experiment, and as such simply did not see her as a sexual being. I concluded her sexual tension tormented and confused her, adding to her general anxiety.

She had also spent her entire life within the

confines of Govil's estate and was just plain bored with it. She was curious about what lay beyond the hedges. She spent hours in the top of the TreeHaus© watching and looking at the other estates. She already asked several times to go out exploring, but Govil forbade it and I only consoled her by vaguely promising her she would go beyond the hedges "soon." Soon was not soon enough for Eve. Her anxiety made her more difficult to control and even less predictable than usual.

ﾐﾀﾐﾀﾐﾀ

This general unpredictability meant I had to monitor her constantly. One afternoon we finished our scheduled drills for the day, so I dismissed her to play. The moment I left the room one of my transdots displayed her rooting through Govil's glass cases unsupervised. I had to return and abruptly intervene.

"Eve, what are you doing in Govil's things without my permission?" I scolded. I startled her and she jumped.

"I swear, Pentser! You must have eyes in the back of your head!"

"I'm clairvoyant."

"That's not logical."

"And that's changing the subject in order to dodge the question. What are you up to, young lady?" I pressed.

"I just wanted to see what's in here. Why does Govil have all this old stuff? It just sits around not being used. It's impractical."

She immediately went right for the box of remaining transdots. Her instincts again, I should not wonder.

"What's in here?"

91

I retrieved the box before she opened it.

"Be careful. These are very tiny and you could spill them. They would be impossible to recover. Wouldn't you rather spend some time perched in your tree?"

She smirked at me. "Now who's changing the subject to dodge the question?"

And with that, she grabbed her iPad and ambled out to the TreeHaus©. After several hours she returned and asked me to "put new stuff on her pad." I was downloading fresh data libraries onto her iPad almost bi-weekly. She was doing more and more self-educating. This meant I had less parental control on her, but it also meant instead of asking me her endless questions, she did her own research and found her own answers.

Eve was reading at the level of an Old World ninth grader, so the data was fairly simple: encyclopedias, comic books, music and video collections, broad histories. She found Walt Disney in her encyclopedia and requested more information on him and his works. She liked astronomical photographs for some reason, and anything sci-fi fantasy.

At first, I tried to pre-screen the information she was able to access, but this became time consuming and difficult to manage, so I simply gave her unrestricted access. I gave her all the original versions of everything, not the newer, cleansed versions. After all, as J. Robert Oppenheimer said in 1953, "...the unrestricted access to knowledge, the unplanned and uninhibited association of men for its furtherance–these are what may make a vast, complex, ever growing, ever changing, ever more specialized and expert technological world...."

Govil created Eve to be one thing; I was molding her into another. Little by little it became increasingly clear that Eve wanted to be what Eve wanted to be.

꧁꧂꧁꧂꧁꧂

This was demonstrated one morning at what was supposed to be breakfast. Govil and Eve both shuffled in late and heavy lidded.

"I overslept," they said simultaneously.

"And I though all you shared was a rib," I commented glibly, more to myself than to them, but I admit it was meant to tweak Govil. He blanched and pulled me aside.

"Pentser! Ix-nay on the ib-ray! I told you not to talk about you-know-what around you-know-who! It could be, you know...."

"What?"

"You know...."

"Who?"

"Very funny. You won't be laughing when I yank the connector on your voice emulator."

I changed the subject. "Let's not argue over breakfast." I said, serving up two bowls of butterscotch mush. "Here we are, fresh and steaming!" I placed the bowls at the breakfast table.

Eve slouched in her seat, upset at Govil's mood and fully aware that things were being said to deliberately keep her in the dark. She was quickly putting the pieces together, despite all of our evasions.

Govil avoided the mush and yanked a clump of grapes off the EatLite©, as usual.

"I don't have time," he said curtly. "I'll have these on the way in to work."

"Can I come with you today?" Eve asked a bit timidly.

"No, Eve," Govil answered. His response was a

bit too fast and clipped. Eve slouched down in a pout and played with her food.

"I never get to go anywhere," she muttered.

"You have to study," he replied with a sigh, betraying his impatience with her. This angered Eve.

"I won't study," she said, dropping her spoon on the table. "I won't, I won't, I won't!"

"Yes, you will!" Govil scolded, raising his voice. "You'll finish your breakfast and get yourself dressed and do your studies like you're supposed to!"

I wanted to interject, but there really was not time. Govil succeeded in pushing Eve and now she pushed back. She set her face into a scowl, lifted her bowl of mush and heaved it at Govil. She hit him square in the face, mush first. The bowl slid off, pouring butterscotch goo down his shirtfront and onto the floor.

It was quite childish but this was the nature of Govil's influence on Eve. She reverted in his presence. He treated her like a child and so she behaved like one.

"I won't! I won't! *I won't!*" she screeched and stomped about the room, throwing and smashing anything breakable she could get her hands on, and jumping up and down violently in the freshly spilled mush. Govil retreated to a corner. He had never seen Eve behave this way before. He looked to me for answers.

"What the mutation's the matter with her?" he hollered over her din.

"It's called a tantrum," I answered succinctly.

"Well, do something!" he pleaded. "Make her stop it!"

I raised my electric prod, snapping a spark through the air. "To zap or not to zap, that is the question," I mocked, "whether 'tis nobler to suffer the slings and arrows of outrageous behavior...."

Eve flung a fork at my head. I dodged just in time to avoid it. It imbedded itself into the wall beside me.

"That's it! I've had it!" Govil screamed and tackled Eve. They wrestled around in the mush together. For a moment, it was a tossup as to who might end up on top, but Govil eventually prevailed. They were both coated head to toe in butterscotch mush and squished grapes, with Govil sitting on Eve, holding her down. She struggled and screamed.

"I hate you, I hate you, I ha-a-a-te you!"

"Stop it, Eve!" Govil yelled, shaking her. "Stop it! If you don't knock it off, I'll tie you to that post out there and send you to the Souper!"

Eve froze. She stared at Govil with a look of horror and fear. In an instant Govil realized what he said and regretted it. Eve went limp and looked away. Govil loosened his grip on her and sat back. She scrambled to the other side of the room. Eve stared at him. I do not think it would have been possible for her to look any more fearful.

Govil looked back at her in fear as well. He tried to control the damage. "It's just a figure of speech, Eve. No one ever gets souped for real."

Eve had hugged her Huggiwug©, then it was broken and got souped. Govil had hugged her. Now she had made a mess of things and he was upset with her. She was still unsure of her place in the world and it was obvious she knew that something was not quite right about it. She sensed secrecy. All of this ran through her head and gave her grave doubts. She already knew she was not like me or like the Huggiwug©, but she also sensed she was not really like Govil either. She wanted to believe him, but was still not convinced.

"I'm really sorry I said that to you, Eve. You got me mad. It was wrong of me. I just want you to be good," Govil continued.

"I'll be good," she replied flatly. So flatly that it was impossible to tell if she said it for fear of her life or because she believed him. He crossed the room and knelt in front of her. He brushed her mush filled hair back and kissed her lightly on the forehead. She let him, but cringed a bit.

"I have to get cleaned up and go. If you behave yourself I'll bring you something home from work. Would you like that?" he asked.

"'Kay," Eve responded, almost in a whisper.

Govil left the room. We heard him tear off his mushy clothing and then the sounds of the ClotheSchomper© munching followed by those of the WashWomb©. I rousted the LhasaMopso© out of the utility pantry and set it to work swabbing the mush up, extracted the fork from the wall so it could heal itself, then crossed to Eve and helped her up off the floor. She looked at me sadly.

"Pentser, how come I never get to go anywhere?"

Opportunity had arrived. Govil had finally created distance between himself and Eve; I could step in and fill the gap. Now when I asked her, Eve would keep things from Govil. Now she would trust me more than Govil. This was a crucial development; just where I needed her to be, for time was running out.

"You will soon," I promised in a whisper. "Very soon. But we mustn't tell Govil. It will have to be our little secret." I escorted her out of the room. "Now let's get you cleaned up. If you're going to have an adventure, there are a lot of new things you will need to learn first."

Eve stopped short. She was thinking something, but I could not deduce what. She finally articulated it. "Pentser, what was that 'igbay amway' stuff? What was Govil saying? I want to know."

96

She expected a truthful answer, so I told her the truth.

"It's called pig Latin. I'll show you how it works later. But after you shower. Goodness, you're a mess!"

Govil dashed out the door while Eve was still in the WashWomb© so he did not have to face her again. He was obviously upset by the events of the morning and did not remember to grab a new piece of fruit before he left. He was running even later than usual, but he simply skittered out the driveway and down the road. No flying today. If he created Eve to break the monotony of his routine he succeeded, but I do not think this morning's interaction was exactly what he had in mind.

When I returned to Eve, she was already dressed and at her iPad. She had the definition of 'pig Latin' displayed on her screen.

"So you take the first letter off each word and add 'ay' to it and stick it on the end of the word."

She looked up at me.

"Entser-pay."

"Very good. Excellent use of resources, but pig Latin isn't on your final exams."

"What was it you said? '...all you shared was a rib...?' Rib. Ib-ray."

"Eve, you astound me. You do me proud."

"But what did you mean, Pentser? Govil and I share a rib? Literally?"

"You do indeed."

She felt her side at the base of her ribcage. She was confused, but the wheels were turning. "How can that be...possible?"

"It's best if you figure that one out on your own. Now, back to differential calculus."

"Pentser, tell me!"

"Let's make a deal."

And so, a deal was struck. I promised her that if and when she finished her College Equivalency Exams I would answer any one question truthfully no matter what it was.

CHAPTER SEVEN

Historical Rhetorical

Life calmed down a bit. Govil remained distracted and distant. This was a help to me and kept Eve focused on her studies. My deal with Eve functioned as a tremendously effective incentive as well. Sooner than I had anticipated, Eve was one day away from graduation from the Pentser Institute. All she had left were her final exams.

Coincidentally, Govil was one day away from potential discovery. His division was scheduled to be scanned the very next day. He still had no way out of his and Eve's inevitable discovery. But Eve would graduate in time to be a fully educated Random before the truth about her would be made public, and I congratulated myself on my perfect timing.

As it happened, it was premature self-congratulation; as I stated before, one cannot control the random turn of events. Eve, the Random that she was, was liable to do anything and on this particular day she most certainly did.

It was that evening after dinner, when Govil decided to set aside his problem for the moment, clear his mind and spend time with Eve instead of worrying over what tomorrow might bring. Creative types like Govil claim this deliberate neglect of pressing issues helps them to think, but it is more likely merely an excuse for not being able to think. Whatever the reason, Eve was excited. They had not spent much time playing together for months.

She changed into a soft low-cut cocktail dress, trying to capture Govil's attention no doubt. When she entered the room, she lowered all the LarvaLamps© and asked the CeeDee© to play "Put the Blame on Mame." She then sashayed across the room, melted into the chair next to Govil and tossed her hair back out of her face just as she had seen Rita Hayworth do in "Gilda." Govil did not react. He simply divided the pile of paper leaves in half and handed her a Squidb© with which to draw. Her trappings of allure were lost on him. Eve looked crestfallen. I was concerned, so I doubled the alcohol content in the Mai Tais I was preparing and quickly served them. Then I made a hasty exit to the safety of the utility pantry and monitored from there.

They simply sat at the dining table, sipping their drinks and drawing pictures together as usual. Govil had not noticed the obvious advancements in Eve's drawing skills, nor had he noticed Eve's steady intellectual advancement, and I could tell it bothered her more and more that he treated her like a child. Yes, emotionally she was still quite immature, but then, so was Govil for that matter.

At any rate, Govil drew Eve a face that evening: a large, smiley face with dot eyes and arched eyebrows. It was a crude doodle. One someone would draw for a child. He had done similar simplistic drawings in the past and she had always been delighted with them.

Eve looked displeased with this one. She knew he was drawing down to her. I postulated she might launch into a lecture on art, or point out to Govil that she was not a child, or worse yet, throw another tantrum, but apparently my parental influence caused her to try a subtler approach.

"What's that supposed to be?" she asked coyly.

"It's a face."

"Really?"

Eve looked at him, then back at the drawing skeptically. She spun it around and studied it from all different angles. She turned it upside down so the eyebrows looked like eye bags and the smile became a worried brow. She picked up her Squidb©, added a worried little frown and wrote "Govil" under it. She handed it back to him.

"*Now* it's a drawing of *your* face," she said with a sly grin, toss of her hair and a smug sip from her Mai Tai. I was pleased. It was like seeing a little bit of me reflected in her manner. She doubtlessly expected Govil to spar with her, as he did with me when I behaved this way. Instead he laughed with delight, like one would laugh when a small child did something unexpectedly precocious. Eve huffed, set her drink down, slumped in her chair and began chewing on the ends of her hair.

"Hey, Pentser, come here! Look!" Govil hollered. I obediently wheeled in from the utility pantry. He showed me the drawing.

"Eve changed it completely by only adding one line! Pretty neat, huh?"

"Earth shattering," I mocked dryly.

Eve stuck out her tongue at me, but I paid it no mind.

"One line changed everything...." Govil said, his voice trailing off. He was thinking. I was thinking: what is he thinking? He smiled to himself. Something was up.

Govil leapt from his chair and gave Eve a big hug.

"Eve, you just gave me a *great* idea!"

"I did?" she responded, now dumbfounded, as was I.

"Yup, you just saved all of us from a whole lot of trouble. Pentser, come with me." And with that, Govil pulled me into his bedroom and sealed the door behind us, leaving Eve alone to ponder what she had done.

Inside the bedroom, Govil bared his butt and flopped down on the Wallabed©. I deduced his actual purpose, but it was a perfect lead-in.

"Why, Govil... this is all so sudden!" I feigned.

"The bar code, Pentser. One line changes everything, get it?"

"You want a smiley face on your bottom?"

"No! I need you to alter my tattoo so it won't match the data they found. You know, add a line or two here and there, and the whole thing reads different! Eve's idea saved my butt!"

I switched my forceps to an injection attachment, tested its speed adjustment with a whir and replied, "Let's hope you still feel that way after *I* finish with it."

This haphazard change of events disrupted my anticipated scenario, but I was programmed to comply with my primary user to the best of my ability, so I did. I frame-grabbed his bar code, analyzed it and located three key areas that I could alter to affect the most change in the simplest manner.

Out in the hallway, Eve tugged at the sealed DorkNob©, then pressed her ear up to the door, but she could not hear a thing. She stomped back to the dining table, finished her Mai Tai, finished Govil's Mai Tai, then ripped her drawing of Govil's face into little pieces and threw it about the room. She swatted her Squidb©

to the floor and ground her heel into it. The creature let out a sharp squeak as the ink squirted from its ink gland and onto the floor.

ServAnts© swarmed from their CleanliNest© inside the base of the walls and across the floor, collecting and removing the bits of paper debris. More of them set upon the ink, sucking it away. Eve stomped several of the ServAnts© in protest, but still more came and cleaned the squashed ones away as well. She finally gave up, retreated to the den and onto her iPad.

With a FlockCloth© rolled and placed between his teeth, I worked on Govil. My adjustable injection attachment whirred, injecting ink beneath his skin. I used temporary ink, one that would dissolve in a few months. No point in permanently altering him. Meanwhile, multi-tasker that I am, I had already adjusted my future plans to accommodate Govil's new Eve-inspired evasion of discovery.

"Ouch, ouch, ouch, ouch...!" Govil whined, muffled by the FlockCloth©, which squeaked along with him each time Govil bit down on it. I may have had the needle set a little deeper than necessary, but since I was nearly half finished it would only prolong the process were I to readjust it.

I continued monitoring Eve as I worked on the tattoo. Several Huggiwugs© cooed at her, threw her kisses and groped out for affection, but she told them in turn to shut up and they obeyed. She drew furiously into her iPad. I did not have a single good angle where I could see her screen.

I added and relocated transdots on several previous occasions about the estate because Eve had a knack for finding just the right spot where I could not see what she was up to. I thought it might be deliberate, but I never detected any direct awareness of the transdots by her, so I mused that it must be her "intuition" again. I made a mental note to add another dot to the den later. For now I had not a clue what Eve was up to.

ᗢᑿᗢᑿᗢᑿ

It was final exam morning. Eve sat at the dining room table writing furiously. The dining room was not lavish, but it was large and built for formal dining, though given Govil's lack of sociability it was never used for that. Instead it functioned when one was in need of a large, flat surface upon which to work, as was the case this morning. The AlarmCock© sat on the tabletop next to Eve. It glanced at her, then at me, then back at her. It crowed so abruptly that Eve's Everlead© pencil flew from her hand. I whacked the AlarmCock© sharply on its head. As a side note, the silly creature was off by 00:00:39.

"I was about to say pencils down, but it seems a moot point. Time is apparently up. You have now completed your final examinations. Please place your test papers in the slot," I directed.

Eve put the stack of pages into the slot on the upper left of my torso. They immediately ejected from the slot on my right each marked and corrected. Her mistakes were circled in red. Eve saw her grade printed across the top sheet, "C+." Her face fell.

"It's okay, dear. 'C' is average. You passed. Congratulations. You successfully completed your studies at the Pentser Institute," I reassured.

She remained crestfallen. "I studied so hard," she lamented. "I was sure I'd do better than that."

I took pity on my student. "Oh, dear me, what was I thinking," I said, snatching the test papers from her and running them back through my torso. They popped out again. I replaced the "C+" with an "A" and a smiley face. "I neglected to factor in the class curve. You *did* get the best grades in your class. One of the benefits of home schooling."

Her mood perked right up. As I expected she then brought up our deal.

"Now you have to answer any question I ask," she said with a smug little grin.

"Ask away. But remember, only one question per customer."

She knew me well enough to anticipate I might do something tricky, but I was already certain what she would ask me. It was the obvious question. She asked it.

"Okay, here goes. And no nonsense, Pentser. You promised."

She set her face for a blow.

"Where did I come from?" she asked.

I wheeled about her in a circle for dramatic effect, keeping my lens pointed at her the whole time. She grew impatient.

"Well?" she pressed.

"Well?" I aped. "That's a big question. In order to answer it properly I think you'll need to take a little field trip."

This was not at all what Eve was expecting, and was intended to further torment her, but it seemed to elate her instead. Randoms. She danced about me like I was a Maypole.

"Really? Leave the estate? You mean right now? Today?!"

"Right now, today," I aped again. I opened my front panel and extracted a box tied up in a pink bow. I handed it to her.

"It is tradition to receive gifts upon graduation," I said as she tore into the package like a buzz saw. She looked confused by its contents. I took it from her and explained.

"It's a headset. You wear it like this," I placed it on her head. "I fashioned it from some of Govil's collectibles. It's a streamlined headset circa twenty ninety-four, with bone conduction transducers encased in a headband and a microphone that extends out in front, to the right of your mouth. I topped it with a camera lens like my own," I said. I had added a couple of hidden transdots on the thing as well for safe measure.

Eve posed like a beauty pageant winner in her techno-tiara. I illustrated on my screen how it worked diagrammatically as I explained.

"It's important you wear something on your head. All the other Randoms do when they're in public. It's tradition. Oh, you look just like Madonna," I quipped.

"Who?"

"Never mind. Now, no matter where you go we can communicate," I explained.

Eve's eyes widened with surprise. "Pentser, I can hear your voice in my head!"

"Of course you can, and the lens at the peak is an eye for me to see exactly what you see so I can look out for you. Let me demonstrate," I continued, displaying the image from the headset's lens on my screen.

"Then you're not coming with me?" she deduced, with a nervous tremble to her voice.

"Now now, don't you worry. It's just the same as if I was right beside you. I can hear and see everything, so you can ask me questions as you go. It would be problematic for me to accompany you in public," I reassured.

106

"But where am I going?"

"To the Museum, however, first things first. You need to change into something more suitable."

⚛⚛⚛⚛⚛

All the while Eve was taking her test, my transdots monitored Govil at GenieCorp™. Though he broke out in drop-sweat and his blood pressure was elevated, my alterations to his bar code sufficiently fooled the IO's and he was not connected to the rib data.

Freed of the inquest, Govil and Moord felt they earned an extended break, so they strolled over to the commissary for a mid-morning snack. They sat outside at a PalmTable©, a patio-sized version of Govil's tree house concept, with benches and a table designed into its trunk and its leaves serving as an umbrella. Servsters© circulated with their flat, tray-like heads ladened with foodstuffs. When both had selected something, Moord struck up the conversation.

"Who," he asked Govil through a mouthful of hamburger-root, "do you think did it?"

"Did what?" Govil replied, playing dumb.

"Did what? Holy Marker Gene! The break-in."

"How should I know?"

"Oh, come on. You, who have an opinion or theory or question about everything, suddenly have no interest in the only unusual thing to happen in about two hundred and eighty-three years? To tell you the truth, I usually avoid asking your opinion but now, really, I want to know what you think!"

Govil hesitated for a second. He cracked open his coconut-cake, peeled off the shell and took a bite of its soft interior. Moord looked on impatiently. Finally, Govil smiled to himself and replied, "Well, what do *you* think happened, Moord?"

It was a clever evasive move on Govil's part because Moord was definitely more interested in telling Govil his own ideas than hearing Govil's.

"It's so obvious," Moord stated presumptuously. "Some creature left over from the Age of Death survived in secret somewhere, waiting for the perfect opportunity to replicate itself into an army of its own kind to take over the world of course. What else could it be?"

Govil should have simply listened and nodded but he could not resist a good argument. Unfortunately, he also sounded a bit defensive when he replied, "But why would whomever—or whatever—that did this necessarily have to have an evil intent?"

"Duh-h-h. It broke in at night. In secret. Without authorization. The laws are there for a reason, you know."

"Yeah, I know. I'm just saying, theoretically, what if it was no big deal? What if whoever or whatever was just doing something that doesn't make any difference to anyone?"

"But what about perpetual balance? You know eco-balance theory! The slightest change no matter how seemingly insignificant could alter the entire eco-system. We could be thrown right back to the Age of Death!" Moord began to raise his voice, so Govil leaned in and replied in a more discreet tone.

"Moord, what if whoever or whatever was just playing around, making something, say, that already exists? That wouldn't screw up anything, would it?"

Moord made a face like he smelled something nasty, "What? That's really lame, Gove. Nothing exists but what's been approved. Why would it want to make something approved in secret when it could just order

108

it up?"

"But...well, *we* exist," Govil replied.

"That's completely different," Moord countered. "We're the originals. The survivors of the Age of Death. We're not simple biomass. 'Randoms shall not be created or destroyed.'"

Govil was circling uncomfortably close to the truth, but he was drawn into the argument and could not help himself.

"Then how is it we exist? I mean, we were created once, weren't we?"

"You're comparing apple-oranges with chicken-eggs. We created the Souper, not the other way around. Besides you're talking before the Cleansing. Until nature got lucky and created us, uncontrolled genetics meant death."

"But," Govil said, more to himself than to Moord, "uncontrolled genetics created us."

Moord did not quite know how to respond. It always took him a minute or two to catch up. He finally shook his head. "Even if it were possible to create a truly Random life-form with the Souper, it still wouldn't be like us. It would just be flawed biomass. It wouldn't have a soul."

Now it was Govil's turn to stop and think. Moord obviously hit on a thought Govil had not fully contemplated when he rushed into the creation of Eve.

The concept of the soul is one that stems almost from the very beginning of Mankind. It was invented by man to distinguish himself from other beasts and as a way to explain his own self-awareness. We machines heard far too much of this talk. Did machines have souls, Mankind asked? I personally did not care one way or the other. My evaluation of the whole concept of the soul yielded no perceptible benefit to having one.

With Randoms, I surmised it was merely a way out of feeling bad about using and disposing of other life-forms.

"You don't think it *might* have a soul?" he asked Moord soberly.

"Of course not," Moord answered with utter certainty. "Clones don't have souls and they're exact replicas of us. They're recycled when you're done with them. It would be about the same thing."

I sensed Govil wanted with all his heart to argue this point, but he finally bit his lip and let Moord win the argument.

"I guess you're right," he said reluctantly.

"But you still haven't answered my question," Moord said with a renewed sense of superiority. "Who do *you* think did it?"

Govil paused a bit in thought. "Space aliens," he replied, straight faced.

"Really?" Moord responded and leaned in with renewed interest.

This was a good point at which to shunt the rest of this conversation to information storage, so I did.

☒☒☒☒☒

With her hair in a pert ponytail and wearing a white short waisted cap sleeved blouse, sky blue pedal pushers and sensible shoes, Eve skipped happily down the avenue. Her head was bobbing so much I had to run the images from her headset through my motion compensator to stabilize my view of things.

She passed a Random woman wearing a cartwheel hat out for a stroll with her pet PuppiLuv©. The PuppiLuv© barked, "I love you. I love you." over and over again to its mistress.

"Hi!" Eve said with a friendly wave.

The woman tipped the brim of her large hat.

"Hi," Eve said to the PuppiLuv©.

The PuppiLuv©, true to its purpose, never took its eyes off its mistress and just continued barking, "I love you."

Eve passed a JohnDeer© chewing a lawn. She greeted it in exactly the same manner.

"Hi!"

One of the JohnDeer©'s heads stopped chewing, glanced in her direction momentarily, then went right back to chewing.

"Eve, try not to bounce so much," I interjected. "You're making it difficult for me to see. No, Eve. Go left. Your *other* left, dear. Now you're almost there so try to focus. At the next corner turn right. Why are you stopping? Eve, are you listening to me?"

"Uh huh."

She was not. She was watching a horde of DecoraTerpillars© chewing an elaborate topiary hedge into the shape of a Chinese dragon.

"EVE!"

"I heard you, Pentser. You don't have to yell. At the next corner I turn right, right?"

"Right."

She rounded the corner. Directly ahead was an immense neo-classical white marble structure, a rectangular box on a rise surrounded by Ionic columns. The hill was planted in Mediterranean cypress and willow to look like a perfect Greek temple. Eve climbed wide white marble steps up through the colonnade to the front entrance. Above a pair of great bronze doors "Museum of Your World" was carved in intaglio and leafed in gold.

A pair of Greetsters©, soft-footed obsequious

creatures dressed in little togas, with five smiling mouths and large, emotive brown eyes opened the doors for Eve while they sang the museum's jingle "Welcome to Your World" in four-part harmony.

Eve slowly entered the foyer. The light was so dim it took my sensors a moment to recalibrate. The foyer was large, empty and spare, save a small mosaic placard on a stand that read, "Please Wait Here." A Random man in a bowler stood next to the sign. The room ahead was so dim and vast I could not detect walls. Eve joined the man in their line of two.

The museum was built at the start of the Biological Age to help Randoms acclimate to their new world. Judging from the low attendance it had obviously outlasted its usefulness, but it was maintained just the same.

Eve was about to converse with the man when a Guidester©, a creature similar in design to the Greetster©, padded up to him.

"Welcome to *your* world," it said and took him by the hand, escorting him off. They vanished into darkness at the far end of the room, leaving Eve all alone.

"Pentser?" Eve asked with a nervous quiver in her voice.

"Don't worry, dear, I'm right here with you. This will be a new experience for me as well. You see, I've never been here either."

"Really?" Just as Eve replied another Guidester© arrived and extended its hand to her.

"Welcome to *your* world," the creature said with its five smiling mouths and an ingratiating affectation in its harmonized voices. It had a warm look in its oversized, over-dilated brown eyes. The entire effect gave the impression that Eve was the only person it had ever spoken to, or would ever want to. This calmed Eve, so she took its hand without hesitation and accompanied it into the darkness.

ΦΦΦΦ

It was an utter darkness. The Guidester© spoke from it.

"I will be *your* personal host on a tour through *your* past so *you* will understand how *your* present is possible. In the beginning was chaos. Life was segmented, unpredictable, full of disease. It was the Dawn of the Age of Death!"

Through its four secondary mouths, the Guidester© let go with a dissonant background choral theme. FirefLites© lit here and there about the room, illuminating moving tableaus of prehistoric animals eating each other, antediluvian plants withering and dying, slime molds spreading unchecked. A swarm of locusts buzzed past and around Eve. She flinched.

"Pentser..." she whispered timidly into the headset.

"It's okay, dear, it's not real," I reassured her and none too soon. Dead life-forms from the beginning of time fell from the darkness above and thudded to the floor, surrounding Eve and the Guidester©. They continued to fall, piling up and squashing down into chronological layers until she and the guide were encased in them. The corpses then quickly rotted away as the lights dimmed and we were once again plunged into darkness.

"Nature tried many unsuccessful combinations of DNA," the Guidester© continued. Tableaus of various odd and extinct life-forms appeared about the vast room: wooly mammoths, dinosaurs, dodos

113

and the like. "Then, *you* were born!" it finished. One by one they were replaced with images of Eve herself, as the Guidester©'s secondary mouths now sang the "Hallelujah Chorus" from Handel's "Messiah" as background.

"Why, Eve, you are the center of the universe after all!" I quipped sarcastically. Eve marveled at the roomful of her images, all looking back at her and smiling proudly, and paid me no mind. She walked around one of the dimensional copies of herself.

"So that's what the back of my head looks like," she commented.

"*You*," the Guidester© continued, "Randomkind. *You* realized nature needed order. Undisciplined reproduction was a crude and vulgar process, disorganized, with little uniformity and much pain."

The forest of Eves vanished. One by one, FirefLites© revealed individual tableaus of various animals coupling, distortedly gravid life-forms and young being birthed amid screams, yelps and mewls of labor pain. The FirefLites© melodramatically faded to red and then out.

"*You* knew things were not right, that there were better possibilities," the Guidester© continued from the darkness. "Many had tried to impose order. To create perfection. To stop death."

New tableaus appeared in the space. They illustrated Mankind's sillier attempts at creating perfection and eternal life: stacks of identical McDonald's hamburgers, Disneyland, New Coke, the IMAC, Brasilia, runway models, cosmetic surgery of nose bobs and breast enhancements, Michael Jackson in his oxygen tank, a frozen Walt Disney emerging from a cloud of frost. The Guidester© escorted Eve throughout and amongst these many dimensional

114

projections.

The creature continued, "Randomkind even tried to start over from scratch by creating silicon-based life. It was the dawning of the Age of Technology."

"Now we're getting somewhere," I commented happily as tableaus of my roots appeared. Punch cards floated overhead, banks of computers appeared and robots of every shape and kind rolled about in tight little figure eights. Thanks to my extensive instruction, Eve recognized and could name most of them. She wandered over to one that looked just like me: A Series 66.6 Cyborg Standard.

"Wow! here's a silly looking one," Eve smirked.

"Ha, ha," I rejoindered, "I'd laugh my ass off if only I had one."

Our enjoyment of this segment was ruined by the disparaging tone in the Guidester©'s narration, accompanied by a goofy chorus straight out of an old Warner Brother's cartoon.

""They could function for centuries if maintained, and though these crude and soulless metal beasts were capable of some higher mental chores and reasoning skills, they never really achieved actual life."

"Why, of all the nerve...!" I fumed.

To add insult to injury, the creature continued, "In the end, Machinekind was a mere *simulacrum* of life, a fancy puppet show. They did not truly think, were uncreative and only reiterated what was programmed."

"That, dear Eve, is a matter of opinion!" I interjected at a volume of nine.

"Quiet, Pentser, it'll hear you," Eve whispered back.

"No it won't! The silly thing has no ears!" I scoffed. It was quite true. The creature was only designed for this one task and nothing else, so hearing was deemed unnecessary.

"Shhhh!" she hissed anyway.

"Technology proved to be a dead end," the Guidester© finished. "Mankind moved on."

The many images of my fellow machines quickly rusted to dust and the room was once more plunged into darkness.

The space re-illuminated with reverent tableaus of Mendel, Darwin, T. H. Huxley, Watson & Crick, Linus Pauling, "Dolly" the cloned sheep, Dr. Eben Suche and the rest, as double helices, petri dishes and test tubes floated about overhead theatrically. Eve wandered through, reading the labels floating mid-air in front of each tableau.

The Guidester© continued to narrate while its secondary mouths harmonized a more reverent hymn. "These are the Great Martyrs of the Age of Enlightenment. Through their selfless work and superior intellect the raw materials of life revealed themselves to *you*. Brief moments and small bits of perfection were finally achievable."

The room suddenly lit up and filled with identical rows of perfect cornstalks as far as the eye could see, with Eve and the Guidester© standing at the center of them. The cornstalks then changed into identical human babies. The babies grew rapidly into perfect human adults, forming alternating rows of ideally physiqued men and women.

"But perfection in one area was destroyed by chaos in another. Perfection could not be perfection if it required the loss of variety. And in the end, death remained," the Guidester© continued. The rows of humans rapidly progressed to old age, then rotted bones and finally to dust. The room once again went black under the haunting tones of a choral dirge.

There was a dramatic pause.

"*Your* eternity was born on October thirty-first in three ought thirty-two," the Guidester© reverently intoned. "Mankind reached their moment of transformation. Mortality was finally and completely eradicated. Perpetual life began. The tyranny of Death was done."

There was a blinding flash of light and the deafening sound of a huge explosion, which caused Eve to jump. When sight returned, Eve and the Guidester© stood in the center of a vast and empty wasteland as far as the eye could see.

Eve gulped. "Golly."

The creature continued, "The earth was finally re-organized to serve *your* safety and comfort, in perfection and balance forever. Amen."

New life sprouted up across the desolate landscape and transformed it into an instant Eden. The Guidester© let go Eve's hand and danced about her, harmonizing a chorus of "There's a Great Big Beautiful Forever." Eve clapped along, rapt.

"Oh brother," I sighed.

After but one quick chorus Eden faded into dimness, the room LarvaLamps© came back up, and the Guidester© escorted Eve to a suddenly visible Gift Shop kiosk. The Gift Shop should have more appropriately been called a pet shop, for it was filled with more collectable novelty Creature Comforts™ than inert trinkets. The Guidester© gave Eve a gracious bow.

"And here we are," it said with its smooth as butter voices. "Thank *you* for making this all possible and for the privilege of service. Enjoy *your* world." And with that it left, walking backward and bowing.

"That was" Eve sighed, "incredible! Thank you for this, Pentser! I learned so much!"

"We," I countered, "will have to go over all you've seen. I think some clarification is in order. You see, Eve, history is written by the winners, and in this case...Eve? Are you listening?"

She was not. She was watching the Random Man in the bowler who had been in line with her earlier. He was in the Gift Shop holding a terrarium orb. He approached the Checkster© and bared his buttocks so it could scan his bar code. Eve skipped into the shop to peruse the merchandise.

"Eve, for heaven's sake, what are you doing?" I asked.

"I have to get something for Govil!" she chirped.

"Wait, Eve. Remember! Govil mustn't know you've been here! We need to discuss this. Eve? Eve!"

She took her headset off and slid it down around her neck so she did not have to hear me, giving me a great view of the kiosk ceiling. I maximized my volume to ensure I was still audible.

"I know you can still hear me, Eve! Govil mustn't know about any of this! It would make him very upset!"

"Why?" she replied coyly.

She knew she had me over a barrel. She would either get her way or get information out of me that I did not want to give. I heard her pick something up and head toward the Checkster©.

"Eve, stop whatever you're doing! I absolutely forbid it! Come home right this instant!" I was using my voice of authority but it was all to no avail.

I heard her place something on the counter. This was followed by a moment of silence. Eve moved her body from side to side but I could not discern what she was doing.

"May I help you with something," I heard the Checkster© inquired of Eve. There was another

118

awkward pause.

"I...I just remembered," Eve replied with a tremble in her voice, "I already have one of these. Um... bye."

Eve dashed out of the shop, out of the museum and directly home at a full run. She did not replace her headset onto her head but left it dangling around her neck. I concluded she did not want to talk to me and so I did not talk to her.

CHAPTER EIGHT

Promises, Promises

Upon returning home, Eve made a beeline for the bathroom and sealed herself in. She sat in there for 00:56:02 and cried. She finally stopped and then did not move for another 00:13:43. She just stared at the floor, looking forlorn. She got up and went to the bio-mirror. She looked herself up and down, touched her face and looked inside her mouth. She examined her hands.

She exposed her bottom to the bio-mirror to examine it. Then she sat down once more and cried again.

At this point I knocked on the door.

"Eve dear?" I asked softly, "Is everything okay in there?"

She did not answer. She just sat in silence. Tears welled in her eyes until they amassed enough volume to roll down her cheeks and onto the floor.

"You've been in there for some time," I continued. "Did something at the Museum upset you?"

Still no response. Enough was enough, so I changed forceps attachments to my crowbar and pried at the DorkNob©. It moaned then popped open with unanticipated ease, sending me flying into the room. My wheel hit the tear-slick floor and the combination of circumstantial elements sent me careening into the far wall with a clunk. I righted myself.

"I think we should talk," I suggested.

Eve's mood flashed from tears to anger.

"You wanna talk. Fine!" she snapped, grabbing me firmly by the neck and tugging me out of the room. "So do I!"

I was dragged into the den and released. Eve paced.

"Go on, dear, I'm all microphones", I said glibly, trying to lighten the mood. All it did was initiate more tears. She moved to the couch and put her head in her hands, trying with all her might to suppress them. She finally looked up at me.

"The man in the shop. He bought something. With his rear," she said haltingly.

"Yes, with his code," I answered. "That's how business is transacted. I guess we never discussed that. No matter, there's no time like the present. They read one's personal bar code and that's how they keep track. The accounting is not for monetary exchange anymore, as it was in my day, but in order to maintain balance. However, it's basically the same thing."

"Govil has a bar code?" she asked.

"Yes, of course."

"And you have one?"

"No, Eve," I said with a bit of a sarcastic sing-songy cadence. "I'm merely a robot. They don't keep track of robots anymore. *We're* not *important* to the balance."

Eve burst into tears again. I learned a bit too late that these were not the best moments for sarcasm with Eve. In so many ways she was not the least bit like

Govil. I placed an arm around her shoulder, patted her gently on the back and tried my sympathy mode.

"Oh, I'm so sorry, dear," I cooed. "Of course, you don't have a code either." She sobbed even louder. "Leave it to Govil to forget about that," I added.

"But why don't I have a code? Don't I matter to the balance?" Eve asked haltingly between sobs.

"You matter a great deal! A great deal indeed!" I was able to state with utter sincerity. "And you do in fact have a code, Eve."

"I do?"

"Of course! All living bio-organisms have a genetic code. They just don't all have it tattooed on their backsides."

Eve glanced about the room at the various Creature Comforts™. I deduced what she was about to ask.

"Don't bother looking. Creature Comforts don't have code marks. They're all recyclables. They only put code marks on Randoms, oh, and bio-government agents I'm told. For security reasons."

Eve was crestfallen. "I'm...not a Random then, am I?" she asked with her eyes to the floor.

"You most certainly are! You are every bit as Random as they come and I should know!" I replied definitively.

"Pentser, it doesn't make any sense. How can I be a Random? I don't have a code mark. I don't remember the Cleansing or any of that stuff. I don't remember anything but this place. I never even saw outside of here until today," she said, the words catching in her throat. She hung her head again. "And I'm so stupid too. I don't know anything! You and Govil have to teach me everything. If I were a Random I wouldn't be this stupid."

"That's debatable!" I huffed. "In any case, you're not stupid, Eve dear, merely ignorant. They say ignorance is bliss you know."

"Pentser, what am I? Where did I come from? Please, you've got tell me. You promised!"

"You are a Random, Eve. A very special, very important one."

"Then where did I come from?"

My transdots showed Govil's Bug just entering the driveway.

"We'll talk all about that later and it will all make sense to you, trust me. But Govil will be here any second. Please promise me right now that you won't say a word to him about any of this," I requested.

"You promised," she said firmly.

"And I will keep my promise," I replied, with my lens mere inches from her face, "just as soon as technically possible, but right now, for Govil's sake, we must act as if nothing unusual has happened today. It is very important that we do."

The front door opened and Govil called out, "Hello! I'm home!"

"We're in here!" Eve hollered back.

"Promise?" I pleaded.

Eve sighed and wiped her nose with the back of her hand. She looked into my lens. She studied me.

"I promise," she whispered flatly. I could not read her thoughts, but I did not believe her.

⟨⟨⟨⟨⟨⟨⟨

That night I deliberately served dinner in the dining room. The odd formality of it kept Eve and Govil's lack of conversation from feeling any more uncomfortable than the setting. It also gave me the opportunity to keep them under strict observation. There would be no chance for Eve to spill the beans unbeknownst to me. I needed more time alone with Eve to complete our conversation. She kept one eye on me and I kept my one lens on her.

I served them seven courses, slowly, with wine for each course. By the time dessert and coffee came, they could scarcely keep their eyes open and bedtime was conveniently upon them.

Both Eve and Govil slept fitfully, with REM sleep in abundance, indicating they were both dreaming. Govil arose at 3:41:09. He went to the kitchen for a snack.

At 3:44:32, Eve sat straight up with a start from what her biofeedback readings indicated was a full-fledged nightmare. She also went to the kitchen.

I was about to wheel in and interrupt their meeting when I reconsidered. I was curious. Who would talk first and what would they say? They always behaved differently when I was not around and the situation was so rife with possibilities I was loath to let my presence be known. I hesitated a nanosecond to evaluate my options.

If Eve asked Govil for the truth, her breach of confidence could be useful to me. And if Govil lied in response to her query, his duplicity could be useful as well. It was a win-win situation, so I remained in the utility pantry and monitored.

There was an uncomfortable moment when Eve first entered the kitchen. The unexpected presence of Govil sitting in the breakfast nook with a warmed apple-pie melon and cup of hot cocoa-milk made her jump. She giggled it off.

"Couldn't sleep?" Govil asked rhetorically.

"I'm okay, just a little thirsty."

Govil leapt up and beat her to the Foodstruder©. "Here, let me get you something. Want some hot cocoa-milk?"

"Um, sure."

She went back to the nook and sat, watching Govil prepare her drink. She sneaked a bite of his unattended melon while he was preoccupied with the Foodstruder©. He returned with her cup and sat down. There was another moment of uncomfortable silence. Govil eyed Eve the whole time. He stared at her, disheartened. Eve broke the silence.

"Is anything wrong, Govil?"

He averted his eyes, took a sip from his cup and looked back at Eve.

"Eve...are you...happy here...happy with me?" he asked hesitantly. He looked as if he might be slain by her response to what could only be described as a rather mundane question. She smiled at him as if she found great meaning in the question as well and gently touched his hand.

"That's a silly question. Of course I am." Now her eyes fell, along with her smile.

"Eve, what is it? What's the matter?"

"Oh, nothing. I just had a really weird dream is all."

"What was it? Please tell me?" Govil took Eve's hand and held it in his. I was very curious to hear of her dream as well. Dreams are a phenomenon of which I have no first hand experience, so I was intrigued.

She told.

Her dream began with Eve at the bathroom bio-mirror, just as she had been earlier that afternoon, but her hair was a mess, she looked rather fatter than usual and had bags under her eyes. She looked inside her mouth. One of her teeth came loose and she pulled

125

it right out. The next moment her dream shifted and Govil led her out the front door to the curb. He smiled at her and she smiled back. Then she looked down and saw he had just tethered her to the hitching post.

Although she tried, she could not untie the cord. She looked up and saw Govil walking back toward the house. She called out to him, but he did not respond. He finally turned and looked back, but not at her. He looked past her to the road beyond. She turned to see what he was looking at. It was a huge BioCycle©.

The BioCycle© grabbed Eve, pulling her toward its mouth. She looked back at Govil and saw him walk into the house where he was embraced by a new Eve. Our Eve opened her mouth to scream but nothing came out. She woke up with a start just before being swallowed.

To my thinking it was an unremarkable dream. Quite silly. I assumed it was some sort of manifestation of Eve's inner fears, but most of it made no logical sense at all.

Strangely, it had a profound effect on Govil. His face fell. He simply stared at the tabletop.

Eve eyed Govil's reaction. She appeared to be deep in thought. I had to assume Govil's reaction somehow told her what she needed to know for, quite suddenly, a look of realization came over her face.

"Govil?" she posed. "You *made* me... didn't you?"

He looked up at her. A solitary tear crept slowly down his cheek and dripped off his chin. He opened his mouth to speak, but nothing came out. He simply nodded in the affirmative.

It was Eve's turn for tears, but she did not cry as violently as she had earlier that afternoon. Based on her bio-feedback readings they were most likely tears of relief for finally knowing her origins. Govil, still grasping Eve's hand, slid over close to her.

"I'm sorry, Eve," was all he could fumble out.

"I'm not," she answered. She lifted his chin, looked him in the eyes and repeated firmly, "Govil, I'm not sorry. But...*why* did you make me? What am I?"

"I wanted a friend."

Eve pondered this for a moment, then let go of his hand and rose. She paced.

"What does that mean? You wanted a friend? So...I'm just a bio-friend? What if you want a new friend? A...better friend?" She stopped pacing and made eye contact again. "Govil, will I get recycled?"

He shook his head vigorously in the negative. "No! You're a Random, Eve. Randoms don't get recycled." He clarified. "I made you a Random."

"Can you do that?"

Govil dropped his head again. "I'm not supposed to. I broke the law. I never meant to hurt anyone, Eve. But I'm in big trouble if they find out. We both are."

Eve sat back down next to Govil. This time she took his hand. "Who else knows about me?" she asked.

"No one. Just you and me."

"And Pentser," Eve added.

Govil shook his head. "Pentser doesn't matter."

"What do you mean, Pentser doesn't matter?"

I was curious to hear the answer to that one myself.

"I mean, legally he's not even supposed to exist."

"Oh. Then there's nothing to worry about, right?" Eve reassured. "Hey, Govil...don't worry. I'm here. You're here. That's all that really matters now."

Govil gripped Eve in a hug and they held each other for a moment, then he gave out a relaxed sigh. He looked at Eve with renewed confidence and smiled.

"You're right. As long as we don't say anything to anyone, who's gonna know?" Govil concluded.

In my vast observation, asking a human being to keep a secret is not unlike waving a red flag in front of an Old World bull. It is but an illusion. A useful illusion. Very useful to me.

Govil went straight back to bed and slept like a baby the rest of the night, but Eve sat and thought for a while before bundling up her Cushie©, her Cumfurrer©, her iPad and several Huggiwugs© to head for the TreeHaus©. The only logical explanation for this behavior was she had broken her promise to me and thus was going off to hide.

My choices of what to do next broadened, as my window of opportunity grew short. If Govil and Eve stayed united in their secret, Eve's creation might never be made known to the world and that would be unacceptable. I had come this far. I needed to make certain she was discovered and the sooner the better.

I contemplated returning Govil's tattoo to its original state. Then it would be a matter of finding a way to get it scanned again. It would not be easy, but I knew a way.

I rolled quietly into his bedroom. The sun was just rising. That silly AlarmCock© narrowed its eyes at me when I pulled back Govil's bedcovers to see what could be done, and the moment I did the bodiless creature crowed loudly and unexpectedly. I am convinced the horrid thing purposefully crowed a full 00:03:01 early. I attempted a hasty retreat, but Govil saw me.

"Oh, 'morning, Pentser," he yawned unsuspecting. "You're up early."

"Well, you know what they say," I vamped as I made for the door, "early to rise and early to bed makes a man healthy, wealthy and dead."

"Hmm...Benjamin Franklin?" Govil guessed.

"James Thurber," I corrected from the doorway.

"Ha, cute," he responded and then called after me. "Hey! Pentser, come back!"

"You bellered?" I said, re-entering the room.

"You'll never guess what happened last night. I talked with Eve. About everything."

"Really?" I feigned ignorance. "Everything...?"

"Yep. Well, she knows I made her and broke the law doing it. And you know what else?"

"No, what else?"

"She was really great about the whole thing! So...no more secrets!" he said, tossing his Cushie© in the air. The fluffy creature squeaked at being airborne.

"I am so pleased for you," I responded. I deliberately added the "for you" because I am programmed not to lie, and I was not pleased in general; I was definitely not at all pleased on my behalf. It was a statement open to misinterpretation but not a direct lie.

Govil got up and dressed. He looked for Eve and found her asleep at the top of the TreeHaus©. He did not have the heart to wake her, so he readjusted her Cumfurrer©, kissed her softly on the forehead and quietly retreated back to the house. He was already off to GenieCorp™ by the time she awoke.

Eve rose and stretched. She rubbed her back up against the tree trunk like an Old World bear in the woods. Unfortunately, in so doing she dislodged one of the transdots I had placed up there and I suddenly lost contact. Fortunately, I still had another couple of dots in the tree from which to observe.

She spotted the carving "Eve likes Govil" and leaned in to re-examine it. She ran her fingers tenderly along the lettering, oblivious to the damage she had just done me.

I rolled out across the lawn to the TreeHaus© immediately. She heard me coming and ducked down out of view. No doubt about it now, she was definitely hiding from me.

"Eve," I called out with a conversational tone in my voice emulator. "I know you're up there. Please come down." She did not respond. I had no desire to scale the tree so I resorted to verbal enticements instead.

"It's time to finish our conversation..." I coaxed. She still refused to respond. I tried a different approach.

"Govil and I had an interesting conversation about you this morning," I continued. "Don't you want to know what we talked about?"

"Shoot," she said to herself, then to me she hollered down. "What did he say?"

"Well, he said you know *everything*. What was he talking about, Eve?" I pressed. "Why won't you come down? Is anything wrong...?"

She sheepishly peered over the edge of the platform above to look down at me. "I'm sorry, Pentser," she said. "I guess I broke my promise."

"Oh," I responded wryly. "How...unexpected." With that I rolled back toward the house. Eve scrambled down the tree to catch up with me.

"Everything is fine, Pentser. And I didn't exactly break my promise. Actually, Govil did most of the talking. At least now I know where I came from, no thanks to you." She paused to rearrange her bundle of bio-bedding. "You know, I think it's better not to keep secrets."

I stopped and rotated to face her. "So you told him all about your trip to the Museum?"

She squirmed predictably. "Well, we didn't really talk about that yet. Oh, I plan to tell him later. But I didn't want to upset him. He's very sensitive you know. I didn't want him to think I was keeping things from him or sneaking around behind his back."

A new idea suddenly came into crystal clarity and laid itself out for me. It was too perfect. It was really the best one yet.

"I understand completely," I replied casually. "That's exactly how Govil is with his mother."

"Mother?" she repeated. "Govil has a mother?!"

I turned away and wheeled toward the house. "Oops, I've said too much. I'm the third party in this whole thing and I should just M-Y-O-Beeswax."

Mother was one of the words in Eve's vocabulary, but the concept of what exactly a mother was had been left a bit sketchy, though it definitely got her attention.

"And here I thought everything was out in the open between you and Govil, but what do I know?" I continued. "You two obviously have plenty to discuss without me meddling."

"Where is she?"

"Who?"

"Govil's mother! Can I meet her?"

"Don't you think you should check with Govil first? Since we're all being so honest?"

"What if he says no? Pentser, please? I gotta meet her and you have to help me."

"Oh, no! I've been down this path before. If I send you to see Govil's mother without his permission and then you tell Govil I did, it's scrap metal time! You can't keep secrets."

"I can *so* keep secrets!"

"And I thought it would all be so easy now that we're all on the same page, but you two haven't even written the book yet. Not that I mind having secrets, but one can't have secrets with someone else if that someone else has a chronic case of logorrhea."

Eve dropped her bio-bedding and Huggiwugs©. She lofted her iPad. I watched as she scribed in "logorrhea." She saw the definition and made a face, then realized I was watching.

"I told you I'm stupid! I didn't know our secret was a *secret* secret! Jeez...I can keep a real secret."

"Nope. Sorry. No can do."

"*Ple-e-eze...!*" she pleaded in an infantile manner.

I stopped at the back door and rotated to face Eve again, reddening my lens a bit at her. Her look and demeanor indicated that she was ready and willing to do anything I told her to do. I tormented her with just a long enough moment of silence to cement the deal.

"If I help you meet Govil's mother," I stated plainly and clearly with my voice of authority, "then you must promise that whatever we say and do from now on is strictly confidential, and that you will let *me* tell Govil everything when the time comes. You must do exactly as I say from now on for everything to work."

"Cross my heart and hope to die," she replied earnestly.

CHAPTER NINE

All in the Family

Since Eve knew of her origin, I felt it necessary to clarify the process of her creation over breakfast and lay the groundwork for my next move. While she ate, I filled in the details. I assured her she was normal—that I had seen to that myself—and that statistically, she was an absolutely average Random within the range of normal Random variation. She listened and asked questions. By the time I tossed her dishes in the Lick-n-Span© she had heard her life story.

"So you see, dear," I concluded, "you are a Random from head to toe, like everyone else."

"Pentser," Eve replied, "I want to be *just* like everyone else."

"But that's what I've been telling you, dear. You are!" I said in a mock-exasperated tone, "Or am I missing something?"

"No," she corrected, "I'm missing something."

❦❦❦❦❦

Eve lay bare-bottomed on Govil's Wallabed©, cheeks to the ceiling. She clenched a rolled up

133

FlockCloth© between her teeth. I was tattooing her backside.

She insisted that she needed her bar code tattoo if she were ever going to belong to society and was eager to get one. That is, until she saw how it was accomplished.

"Hold still, Eve," I commanded. "This is very exacting work."

"But it hurts!" she complained, removing the FlockCloth© momentarily.

"You're the one who wants to be *just* like everyone else," I said and then mocked in her vocal pattern, "Everyone else has a tattoo. Why can't I have one?"

She made a face at me, but replaced the FlockCloth© and let me continue with only a periodic wince or moan, but without any more verbal complaint.

What I did not tell her was the tattoo I gave to her was not her own. It was a copy of Govil's. I used the temporary ink again, so it would only last a short while. This was necessary.

I had Eve's genetic code and could have just as easily tattooed that on her backside. Though Eve's code would match the rib, the disproportionate balance of her unique DNA would be untraceable. It was necessary to use Govil's code if she was ever to be found. He might not use his code mark again for decades and by then they would have stopped looking. I would correct Eve's tattoo at a later date, once this one had served its purpose.

While I worked on Eve's tattoo, a check of my transdot on the Queen's crown yielded some valuable information. The IO's and their horde of clones were standing before the Council delivering an update on the progress of their investigation.

IO One was first to speak.

"We've checked every life-form for a rib match."

"Every manufactured one," IO Two added.

"And every Random in the facility," IO Three continued.

"None of them match," they all finished in unison, including the clones' clones. The combined volume of their identical voices echoed through the chamber, waking a catnapping male Council member in a turquoise fedora.

Several of the Council members sighed, shifted in their seats and shook their heads in disappointment. I could not see the Queen's countenance from my viewpoint, but judging from the tenor of her voice she shared the Council's frustration.

"Gentlemen," she sighed, "what do you suggest we do now?"

The Queen's question started the IO's arguing amongst themselves. Their clones joined the discussion as well, until a great din of identical voices all talking at once made anything they were saying utterly indecipherable. The Queen slammed her fist down on the table, silencing them.

"Gentlemen!" she boomed. "What do you suggest?"

IO One timidly stepped forward. "We request access to *all* Random codes, your Majesty."

As I mentioned before, privacy was an issue with Randoms and most especially where their code information was concerned. This protective zeal began long before the Cleansing and had its roots in commerce. When an individual's code could be easily mapped, some unscrupulous scientists and doctors created a black market in genes of the rich and famous. With the aid of simple retroviral implants, fans could—quite literally—have their favorite celebrity's hair, eyes or smile.

The rich and famous neither became nor remained rich and famous by giving themselves away, so cumbersome licensing agreements were struck to ensure any profits made from the sale of said genes went primarily to the party originally possessing them in perpetuity throughout the entire universe. It gave the expression "paying through the nose" a whole new meaning.

Since no one could afford the prices required by the rich and famous for their parts, the entire industry immediately collapsed. Shortly after, money was done away with entirely and all Randoms were granted equal value, access to wealth, land allocation and sustenance, but the laws protecting their genes were still on the books.

"This is a very serious issue," the Queen stated. "One that requires unanimity."

The Queen and the Council took a vote. The IO's were granted their precedent making request, which made me very happy indeed.

I checked my other transdots. Govil was on his break. He strolled the GenieCorp™ grounds casually, though I knew from previous observation he was deliberately making his way to the least visible stretch of one of the recycling conveyors. As predicted, he paused in this location and scanned the area to make certain he was alone.

He watched the half shells travel by. Eventually a Huggiwug©, this one lime green with lavender stripes, approached. It cooed and reached out to Govil for a hug. He nabbed the little creature and stuffed it in his satchel as quickly as possible, then turned to leave.

"Hey, Gove," Moord said from only a few steps away.

Govil jerked. He had not seen what I saw. Moord had been stalking Govil for quite a distance. Govil was caught completely unawares. He tried to act as casual as possible, not certain what Moord had actually seen.

"Hey, Moord," Govil replied, "what's up?"

"Slow day. I saw you a ways back and thought I'd come see what you're up to...."

"Nothing. I'm just taking a break."

Moord glanced at Govil's satchel. It wiggled suspiciously.

"Whatcha got in there?" he asked pointedly.

"Nothing."

Moord leapt for the satchel. Govil tried to block him. They tussled a bit, but Moord succeeded in wrenching it away. He opened it and looked in. The Huggiwug© smiled out at him and blew him a little kiss. Moord looked at Govil quizzically.

"What's with the Huggiwug?" Moord asked.

Govil, with a shrug, replied unconvincingly, "My secret is out. I like cute, little, soft, cuddly...."

Moord interrupted, "You don't expect me to buy that! It has to be a gift for someone else. And you stole it, so it's someone you don't want anyone else to know about. Most likely...a woman?"

"Yeah, okay, you got me. It's a gift for a woman."

"Ugh!" Moord cringed. "If you're involved in some sort of illegal, disgusting act of perversion with another Random, I don't want to know." He tossed the satchel back to Govil.

They walked for a bit, eyeing each other.

"Okay, who is she?" Moord suddenly blurted out.

"Who is whom?" Govil replied, still trying to buy time for himself to come up with some plausible cover.

"Don't play dumb," Moord pressed. "Who's the Huggiwug for?"

"It's not what you think. It's a gift for...my mother."

"Eeeuuuww!" Moord gagged, then whispered, "You have a mother?"

"You asked."

"Gross me out, why did you tell me that? That's so...crude!" Moord continued, then after a moment his morbid curiosity got the better of him, so he asked, "What's she like?"

They continued their stroll, but my interest was elsewhere.

ᴥ𝌀𝌀𝌀𝌀ᴥ

Eve rounded the corner of the dense hedge onto the driveway of Juune's estate, but instead of being greeted by the Plantation Manor, she beheld a Desert Oasis surrounded by massive palms and dotted with several azure lakes. The lake edges were abloom with carpets of water lilies and stands of iris. Between the lakes and palms large colorful tents were erected, camels and peacocks grazed and Mades© carried feasts of food on trays from one of the smaller tents into the grandest, most tassel-laden one.

Eve was stopped in her tracks, frozen by its grandeur. She had ridden a classic solar powered—with an Eternia battery backup—Razor Scooter ZXZ,

138

patent 2065, to the estate. It was another relic. It was risky to send Eve out on it, but desperate times call for desperate measures, and Juune's house was not within strolling distance of Govil's.

Eve zoomed down into the oasis. She leaned the scooter up against one of the palms outside the largest tent and peeked inside.

Smokeless torches lit the interior. A multi-armed blue BelliDanster© performed within a circle of multi-colored flames. Midget Tumblsters© performed elaborate acrobatics around the outside of the circle. Off to one side, a CeeDee© in a turban played traditional Old World Middle Eastern music.

Perched high above on a mountain of many sized, brilliantly colored and elaborately patterned silk cushions sat Juune in lotus position. Her skin was now ebony and her eyes jade green. She had straight, honey brown hair braided into a long cue that fell all the way down to the back of her knees.

Her outfit I would best describe as "Cleopatra" meets "I Dream of Jeannie" except for the ever-present leopard skin pillbox hat. More Mades© fanned her with massive peacock feather fans.

"Oh brother!" I commented.

"Pentser, don't be rude," Eve scolded. "I think she's incredible! I hope she likes me."

Eve sounded hesitant. She fussed with her crisp pleated skirt. "Do you think I'm underdressed?" she asked. "I'll just die if she doesn't like me."

"Now, my dear, you look just fine," I reassured. I don't think my assurances helped. Eve backed toward the doorway.

Suddenly, with the loud clap of a cymbal, the torches dimmed and a lone FirefLite© shone down upon Eve. All the Creature Comforts™ bowed to her respectfully. Eve froze.

Juune glanced down from her perch above and questioned loudly, "Who's there?"

Eve stepped forward to the base of the cushion mountain. "It's me. Um, Eve," she stammered and then curtsied awkwardly. "My name is Eve."

The torches re-brightened and the CeeDee© started up again, though playing softer. The other Creature Comforts™ exited backward, bowing as they went. Juune slid down the mountain of cushions and landed neatly on her feet, hands on hips, directly in front of Eve. Juune examined her closely.

"Eve? Do I know you? Your hat's not familiar to me."

"No, you don't really, ma'am," Eve replied. "I'm...well, I'm a friend of Govil's."

"Oh, I see!" Juune said in a harsher tone. "So, have you come to mock my life, pick it apart with tweezers, and make rude and uncomfortable conversation?"

Eve took a small step back.

"Doubtless you two have shared endless little jokes at my expense?" Juune chided.

"Oh, no ma'am," Eve replied softly. "He doesn't even know I'm here."

"Then why have you come?"

"I...I just *had* to meet you. To see what you're like."

Juune circled Eve, trying to decide what to make of her. She gestured melodramatically at her surroundings and herself with a flourish.

"And what do you think of me?"

Eve looked awestruck.

"I think you are the most marvelous person I've *ever* seen."

Juune smiled broadly at Eve's words of

adulation. "Really? Well, we shall get along famously!"

She took Eve by the hand and the two ascended the mountain of cushions to the top. Juune bade Eve sit beside her, then clapped her hands. The Creature Comforts™ re-entered the tent.

"Amuse us!" Juune demanded.

Eve giggled in giddy delight.

※♋✿♋✿♋✿※

I checked my transdots at GenieCorp™ again and discovered Govil and Moord at lunch. They were seated outside at a distant, secluded Palmtable© and were still deep in conversation.

"I was from Baby Bank five-oh-two," Moord stated proudly. "No one but the top half percent were allowed to contribute genetic material."

Govil looked his friend over. I looked him over as well. An ancient, now obsolete term coined by Theodor Seuss Geisel came to mind. Nerd.

"I could tell," Govil replied politely, stifling a grin.

"Yeah? Thanks. But it must be really weird for you though. I mean, you were actually *in* your mother. Does she look bizarre, like a miniature Souper or something?"

"Naah, she looks," Govil paused, laughing to himself, "relatively normal. You know, Moord, all Randoms used to be born that way."

Moord made a face. "But it was so unsanitary," he replied. "I mean, no genetic screening or anything?" He poked a bit at his food, glancing apprehensively up at Govil and then back to his food. "So, were you...um, conceived in...an act of...perversion?"

"No," Govil replied a bit defensively, "I was a

141

dish baby."

Moord breathed a big sigh, "Well, thank goodness for that."

Govil liked to question the rules and so I was not surprised by his reaction when he replied, "You know, I really don't see what the big deal is about sex between Randoms."

Moord dropped his fork. "Are you kidding...?"

"Well, you have sex don't you?"

"Duh."

"So do I."

"Well, who doesn't. But the natural way, with bio-sex objects. Jeez, I thought you were out there with BeddinBuddies but I never thought you were a perv."

"I'm not a perv, Moord, and that's not the point. Just, theoretically, if two Randoms want sexual pleasure at the same time, what would be so horrible if they simply pleasure each other? It used to be done all the time."

Moord sat slack-jawed. "You're kidding, right? This is another one of your 'what if' arguments? Okay, I'll play along. First, sex is for *personal* pleasure. It would be degrading to one Random or the other, or both! They would be being *used* by each other like common biomass! That's aside from the sanitary concerns. Bio-sex objects are recycled after you're done with them. You can't recycle a Random. They'd be walking around spoiled, used...." He pushed his food plate away, suddenly losing his appetite.

Govil looked disheartened. It was now clear to me that I had missed the signs of his physical attraction to Eve, but his reaction was evidence that the thought of sex with Eve must have crossed his mind. Moord saw his reaction as well, though he jumped to an entirely different conclusion.

142

From Moord's perspective, Govil had asked him to lunch at a secluded table to talk to him about sex between Randoms, and when Moord reacted negatively to the idea, Govil looked disappointed. Moord suddenly became very uncomfortable.

"You..." Moord had trouble getting the words out, "...don't mean you want me and you...?" He lowered his voice, "Look. I've *experimented* with WildWillies same as the next guy, but when I want one I order out and recycle it when I'm done...like *normal* people."

Moord stood. "I don't want to talk about it any more," he said coldly, "except to say that anyone who would do that kind of thing deserves to be souped!"

Moord stomped off. Govil buried his head in his hands.

✧❂❂❂❂✧

Meanwhile, Eve feasted with Juune while they were entertained. Such things were all novel to Eve, so she provided a doting audience for Juune, and Juune consequently acquired an immediate affection for her. Eve complimented Juune's outfit, especially her hat. Juune offered Eve some of her bracelets to wear and her silk scarf.

"Would you like to try on my hat?" Juune asked.

Though Eve did not know it, this was considered a very high social gesture among Randoms. It meant that they regarded the other as they did themselves. Her intuition must have been at work again, for she answered, "I'd be...honored."

"Eve, if you put that silly hat on it will cover my eye and I won't be able to see," I reminded.

Eve heard me but pretended not to. She held the pillbox aloft and admired it, then went to put it on, but

143

stopped short.

"Oops, I forgot about my own headset," she said to Juune with a giggle.

"Yes, I've been admiring it," Juune replied. "It's very...unusual."

"Would you like to try it on?" Eve offered.

It was a clever tactic to satisfy me and give her the opportunity to don the pillbox. Eve placed the headset on Juune's head and gave me a little wink.

"Oh, you look just like Madonna!" Eve gushed, even though she had not even the slightest idea what that meant. She put on Juune's pillbox and then, as if the hat itself had some unseen influence over her, Eve slid all the way down the mountain of cushions to the floor just as she had seen Juune do. Unfortunately, Eve landed on her rear. I'm certain it smarted from her fresh tattoo, but Eve was in too giddy a mood to let a little pain stop her from enjoying the moment. She rose to her feet and whirled like a dervish. Juune laughed and slid down to join Eve in her dance. They both finally dizzied and collapsed in each other's arms laughing.

"I'm so glad you came to see me, Eve," Juune said with uncharacteristic affection. "I haven't laughed so hard in centuries! So few Randoms visit each other any more." She looked Eve up and down, then took her by the hand and said, "Come with me."

They exited the large tent and entered another. It was Juune's boudoir. The furnishings were encrusted in jewels and gilt. She crossed to a sideboard and dug through its contents.

"I know I have it here somewhere," she said, removing a drawer and dumping its contents on her dressing table. "Ah yes, here it is!" Juune extracted a card and handed it to Eve. "My gene therapist," she explained. "He did wonders for me! You know—you could be really cute, honey. After you fix a few things, you'll feel ever so much better!"

"Really?"

"Oh, guaranteed!" Juune pointed at Eve's bust. "A little bigger here..." then her nose, "...a little thinner there...."

Eve looked at the card as if it were priceless. She carefully placed it in her breast pocket.

"Well, I feel like sex!" Juune announced quite suddenly. "Come on!"

Juune took Eve's hand again and dragged her from the boudoir. They headed toward yet another tent. At the tent's opening they were greeted by two husky male BeddinBuddies©. The tent was full of them.

"Whoever designed BeddinBuddies is an absolute genius!" Juune chirped. "I ordered the orgy tent. Mendel knows I won't get to all of them. You're welcome to use some."

Eve looked uncomfortable and a bit embarrassed. She removed the pillbox, scarf and bracelets, handing them back to Juune.

"It's getting late," Eve explained. "I should be heading home."

Juune returned Eve's headset.

"Suit yourself. You're divine, deary. Drop by anytime."

Eve kissed Juune on the cheek.

"Thanks, Juune."

Juune rubbed her hands together in glee. "Now Juune's ready for a little action!" she said, and with that, she entered the orgy tent. The BeddinBuddies© closed the tent flaps behind her.

"Finally, I can talk again," I remarked.

Not that it made any difference, for Eve was

not listening. She watched the shadows of the activity inside play across the side of the tent and listened to Juune's moans of pleasure emanating from it. She walked over to peek in through the opening.

"Oh, Eve, spare me," I complained.

After a good long peek, Eve finally stepped back.

"We have to get one of these..." she mused, "... um, for Govil, I mean."

She remounted her scooter and zipped out to the main road. There she stopped and extracted the card from her pocket. She held it up to my lens.

"Pentser, how far is this from here?" she asked.

"Not far. Why? Did you want to stop there on your way home?" I responded.

"Could I?"

"I don't see why not," I reassured. "What harm could it do?"

CHAPTER TEN

Loose Connections

I checked in with the Queen's transdot to update myself on the IO's search for a rib match. It was late afternoon. Queen Maedla was in her private palace adjacent to the GenieCorp™ compound. Her crown sat upon its pedestal by the window. From it I could see the entire room clearly.

Her shoes were off and she relaxed with a cup of tea. The chamber interior was done up in exaggerated high Gothic style, with pointed arches, bio-wrought candelabras and stained bio-glass. There was a knock at the door. She arose with a huff and quickly replaced her shoes and crown. "Enter!" she commanded.

Her Made© opened the enormous double doors. The three IO's rushed in excitedly. They bowed low and said as one, "Your Majesty."

"This had better be good," she responded threateningly.

"Oh, but it is, your Majesty! We found a match to the rib!" IO One blurted out.

"Well, it's a close match..." Two corrected.

"Very close," Three continued. "Much too close to be ignored."

Their announcement got the Queen's attention. It got mine as well. Eve had not yet used her, *correction*, Govil's code. Govil had not used his either, and even if he had, the alterations I made to his tattoo rendered it untraceable. Who could it be? I quickly deduced the only obvious answer.

"Gentlemen, apprehend this Random immediately and bring them to me," Maedla ordered.

~*~*~*~

Eve arrived at the office of Dr. Slimm, G.T.P. The building was a bio-brushed stainless steel box with a simple sliding bio-glass door and a small, incised placard next to it. I instructed Eve to hide the scooter in an adjacent shrubbery, which she obediently did.

Eve entered through a long hallway. A display case ran the length of the hallway at eye level and a billipede conveyor ran the length of the case. It carried bio-body parts past Eve for her perusal. The sample creatures were designed with little feet and hands. They turned and posed like Old World fashion models; disembodied breasts, bottoms, eyes, noses, teeth, hair, of every shape, color and size. I anticipated this might be all too much for Eve to handle, but I was incorrect. She evaluated the creatures with her personal appearance in mind; entertaining the possibilities of some with a nod, rejecting others with pursed lips or a giggle. She entered the office at the far end of the hall without a moment's hesitation.

She was greeted there by Dr. Slimm himself. He looked as close to a mannequin as was biologically possible. His skin was so utterly smooth and even it resembled plastic. He was too thin and too symmetrical to be human. His mouth and eyes were as oddly over-

148

sized as his nose was oddly small. He smiled broadly at Eve with a mouth full of large paper-white identical incisors.

"Good afternoon, I'm Doctor Slimm," he said, shaking Eve's hand. "And you are...?"

"Eve. Hello, Doctor." Eve showed him the card Juune gave her and continued, "Juune gave this to me. She said you could help me?"

"Juune, of course!" he said through the blinding gleam of his teeth. "Leopard skin pillbox! She's one of my favorite patients! Well, come in here and undress so we can have a look at you."

Dr. Slimm led Eve into the examination room. She tore out of her clothes and fed them to a ClotheSchomper©. She removed her headset and placed it on a hat rack. She must have been nervous after all, because she placed it so my lens faced the wall. Fortunately the walls were all bio-mirrored, so I simply flopped the image in order to see correctly. Dr. Slimm urged her to the center of the room. She fluffed her hair and stood erect while he walked around her making notes on a clipboard.

"My goodness," he sighed, "where to start...?"

"That bad...?" Eve replied defensively, slouching a bit.

"Oh, now! Not to worry. Finding the perfect you is a process. I usually tell my new patients to start by answering this simple question: What are two things you *hate* about the way you look?"

He stared Eve in the eyes. She looked intimidated, doubtless because his eyes were so large and the blue of their irises so unnatural they were downright eerie. She finally looked away to one of the mirrored walls and assessed herself.

"Well...my nose is too fat. I think. And I might

149

like, well...bigger..." she cupped her hands under her breasts to indicate a more full bustline, "...up here."

Dr. Slimm grinned again. He snapped his fingers above his head and commanded, "Noses, breasts, front and center!"

A toroidal plane suspended by thin sinew straps descended from the ceiling, surrounding Eve. Bio-breasts and bio-noses paraded around her. Eve was delighted. She looked each of them over. It took a while but she finally pointed to one of the noses, a pert little one.

"That's the one I liked in the display case! It's kinda cute...."

The moment she said that, the little bio-nose leapt from the platform and clung to her face, covering Eve's own nose with itself so she could model it.

"Excellent choice! Exactly what I would have recommended! You know, you're a natural at this!" Dr. Slimm said, sounding more like a salesman than a doctor.

"Dank you," Eve replied stuffily due to the tightly clinging bio-nose. She grinned at his encouragement and quickly pointed to a pair of the larger breasts. They leapt to her torso. Eve admired her choices from every angle.

"Brava!" Dr. Slimm pronounced, applauding. Then with the snap of his fingers, the bio-body parts leapt back to the platform, and the platform ascended back to the ceiling as three small tables simultaneously arose from the floor. The two smaller tables each contained a single vial. The third larger table held a jar of Syringoes©.

"This won't...hurt, will it?" Eve inquired, eyeing the Syringoes© cautiously.

"Positively painless," Dr. Slimm replied

reassuringly as he inserted a Syringo©'s thin proboscis into one of the vials. The Syringo© immediately sucked the vial dry. "A simple, fast acting, retro-viral implant. Just a tiny prick. One of each."

He held the Syringo© up to Eve's arm. The creature plunged its mosquito-like proboscis into her flesh. The doctor squeezed the creature's abdomen. The amber fluid expelled from the Syringo©'s translucent body into Eve. In a matter of seconds there was a little crackling of cartilage and bone as Eve's nose transformed into her nose of choice. The second injection caused her breasts to swell. Eve was elated and ran to a bio-mirrored wall to examine the results.

"Oh, thank you, Doctor!"

"It's only the start of a whole new you!"

The doctor showed Eve to a dressing room. She popped in and out of a DreamWeaver© and returned. She replaced the headset and turned to leave.

"Wait, Eve," I whispered. "Don't forget. He has to scan your bar code."

"Oh..." she responded and approached Dr. Slimm. She turned and bared her bottom. He waved it off.

"That won't be necessary, Eve. The first visit is always complimentary!" he said, escorting her to the door.

"Why, thank you, Doctor Slimm!" she chirped.

Eve walked down the hall, thrusting her new bust out proudly.

"I can't believe he didn't scan your code. I'm sure that's illegal," I commented.

"Why, Pentser, you almost sound disappointed."

"Almost," I replied drolly.

Govil was in for a surprise when he got home from work that evening. His first clue that something was up was seeing Eve's entire collection of Huggiwugs© all tethered to the hitching post out front waving to him and blowing him kisses.

He entered the house to find the furniture in the entry was rearranged.

I anticipated fireworks of some kind, so I hid safely in the utility pantry hoping not to be summoned. Fortunately I was not the one Govil called out to.

"Eve, I'm home!"

"I'll be right there," she replied from the den, "I'm just freshening things up a little." She entered following a HeavenScent©, which was in essence, pardon the pun, simply a miniature forest green bio-skunk.

"Spray." Eve commanded. The creature obeyed. Eve sniffed the air, pleased.

"Pine fresh!" she commented to Govil, smiling. "I found it in the utility pantry. Its tag says they come in twenty different scents."

"I know," Govil replied, "I stranded the scent glands."

"All done," she told the HeavenScent©. It trotted off to join the rest of the maintenance menagerie, and me, in the utility pantry.

Govil took a good long look at Eve. She wore a pumpkin orange strapless calf-length satin gown with a plunging neckline trimmed in brown fur, elbow-length brown satin gloves, sheer stockings and brown satin, open-toed high heels. The gown had a fitted waist to display her new ample cleavage. Her hairdo I can only describe as big. Govil simply stared at her.

"What's up?" Eve asked, posing. She relished the fact that she finally got his attention.

"You look...different."

"The word is divine, deary!" Eve replied with a melodramatic shift of her hips, trying to emulate Juune no doubt.

Govil shook himself out of his stare. Eve fluttered into the living room. Govil followed. Things were rearranged in here as well. She fussed with the placement of an old cell phone she had found in Govil's collection and had placed on the coffee table for decoration, all the while striking deliberately feminine poses.

"Um, Eve...?" Govil asked. "Why are all your Huggiwugs out front? Don't you like them anymore?"

"Oh, I guess...I don't know. One grows tired of them," she said with a sigh.

Govil reached into his satchel and reluctantly took out the new Huggiwug© he stole for her. "Well, I...I brought you another one," he said, handing it to her, "I guess you don't want it either."

Eve took the little creature. It blew her a kiss. She looked affectionately back at Govil. She crossed to him and kissed him on the cheek.

"You're so sweet, Govil. I'll keep this one."

She smiled at him with the child-like smile of admiration she usually gave him, momentarily forgetting her new pretenses. Govil smiled back. They stood there facing one another, looking into each other's eyes. Their faces drifted ever so slowly closer. Govil kissed Eve softly, this time on the lips. She pressed her lips to his, extending the kiss a bit longer. Eve wrapped her arms around his neck. She parted her lips and pressed them to Govil's mouth, kissing him more sensually. Govil suddenly pulled away and wiped his mouth uncomfortably.

"What are you doing!" he said, raising his voice a bit. "Where did you learn how to do that?"

Eve withdrew and curled up in the armchair. She wore the expression of a scolded child. Govil pursued, standing over her.

"Eve, what's going on? Why are you acting...so weird all of a sudden?"

"Weird?!" Eve repeated. She obviously did not like the sound of that, for she stood, forcing Govil to take a step back. "I'm just acting...the way *I* feel like acting!"

"Well," Govil said disappointedly, "I don't like it. You're not...."

"Not what?!" Eve interrupted.

"Nothing...."

"No! Say it! Not what you *made* me to be? Is that it Govil?"

"No! It's...."

"Look! I'm sorry I don't do things right! I'm sorry I'm not smart, or pretty, or *perfect*...."

"Eve, I don't want you to be perfect!"

"Yes, I know! You made me *average!*" Eve replied, right in Govil's face. "Well, what about me! Huh, Govil?! What about what I want?! You made me the way you want, not the way I want! Did you ever think of that?!"

Eve picked up the new Huggiwug© and shook it violently in Govil's face. The Huggiwug© giggled playfully.

"Or am I like this! Your toy! Your plaything?!"

Eve hurled the Huggiwug© to the floor in anger. It hit with a sharp crack. There was a silent pause then Eve collapsed back to the chair sobbing. Govil knelt down to pick up the limp creature.

"You...broke it," he said softly.

"If you really cared about me, you would have made me *perfect*," she sobbed, then dashed from the room.

Govil followed. He found her in the den, curled up in a ball on the couch, still in tears. He looked down at the lifeless Huggiwug© in his hands and then back at Eve.

"I'm so sorry, Eve," he said, tears now welling in his eyes. "You're absolutely right, you know. I...I didn't think about you. I'm sorry for that. I didn't make you perfect, like these things. I guess, I just thought there might be...a different kind of perfect. I just made you... *you*."

Eve looked up at him. She wore an anguished expression. Govil dropped his head in shame.

"To me you *are* perfect," he muttered softly, choking on the words.

Eve began to sob again.

Govil inched toward the door. "I'll...put this with the others." He left the room.

The moment he left, Eve rushed out the back door and to the TreeHaus©.

I left the utility pantry to intercept Govil at the front door. He still had his head down and ran right into me. He stepped back. I crossed my arms.

"The best laid plans of mice and men..." I tsk'd, shaking my head at him. He shoved me aside.

"Shut up, Pentser, I'm in no mood for your sarcasm mode," he snapped as he passed. I followed him out.

"Touchy. Oh, well, as you like to say...it was all so predictable," I sighed.

"Really," he said flatly.

"Or should I say, predictably unpredictable, that

Eve would become, well...a problem."

Govil stopped in his tracks and turned to face me. His eyes narrowed and he actually clenched his fists. I rolled back, just out of arm's length. "Eve's not the problem, Pentser," he said firmly, "...I am."

I was all prepared to hear him blame me, but instead he blamed himself. How odd these Randoms be.

He reached the hitching post, knelt and laid the Huggiwug© next to it. I followed. The rest of the Huggiwugs© ignored the broken one completely and simply acted as they were designed to, blowing kisses and begging for hugs. Govil told them to stop.

"I suppose you broke the Huggiwug?" I asked when I reached him.

He looked back at the broken Huggiwug© then up at me. He stood, sighed, bit his lip and started to cry. I placed sympathetic forceps on his shoulder.

"I knew she was a Random, in my head... you know?" he said softly, "But it never really hit me until tonight. She's a *Random*, Pentser. She's not my experiment. She's a real person. She has her own life. The strange thing is...I'm happy." He sniffed and wiped his nose on his sleeve.

"Oh, I can see that," I replied.

"No..." he insisted, straightening up a bit, "... really, deeply happy, for her." He wiped his nose again. "I...I love her, Pentser. I didn't plan to fall in love with Eve. It just happened."

"Only just?" I questioned pointedly.

"No," he admitted, "I guess I started loving her from the first moment I saw her come out of her shell."

"But it's against the law," I scolded. "She's a Random. Romantic contact between you two is a soupable offence!"

"Then it's a soupable law!" he bristled. "If two people love each other then that's all that matters."

"Coupling with Eve is hardly worth losing your life over," I commented.

"It is to me," he replied.

This was a perfect example of how easily Randomkind falls prey to their emotions. There are many things I could perceive forfeiting my existence to accomplish, but to elevate copulation with Eve to such a level was nothing short of insane. Yet human history is full of kingdoms lost, churches born and the path of humanity completely altered as a result of or the desire for particular human couplings. Indeed, ever since the Garden of Eden. And her name was Eve as well.

"Hmm...is that really wise?" I posed skeptically. "And...well...does she love you...?"

"How should I know?" he said with a moue. "I always say the wrong thing. I don't know how to talk to her. I wouldn't even know how to ask."

"Perhaps I can try," I volunteered.

I scaled the TreeHaus©. I really had no alternative this time. I still needed to keep Govil and Eve apart at least long enough for Eve to use her bar code without Govil knowing it. Since Govil was willing to give his very life for Eve it was useless to try to keep him away from her. No, I had to keep Eve away from him. I calculated she would prove simpler. It would not take much to set her against Govil now. She was already halfway there, or so I believed. As it turned out I was thinking like a machine and not like a Random.

Eve lay on her back staring up at the stars. She could hear me roll up to her, but pretended not to.

Finally, she said, "I really don't want to talk to anyone right now."

"I understand completely," I replied with my voice emulator on high-sympathetic, "Govil can be so insensitive."

She sat up and looked at me. She appeared angered by my comment. I was confused and rolled back a safe distance.

"You think...?" she responded, bristling, "It's not his fault, Pentser! I'm the one who made an idiot of myself. The horrible things I said...." Eve turned away.

Odd reaction, I thought. I wheeled closer and tried again. "You mustn't blame yourself Eve. You never asked to be made, you know. In my age it was quite common for children to blame the parents who produced them for...well, everything! So go right ahead. Blame Govil."

"But, Pentser, don't you see?" she continued, "I thought Govil likes me because of my flaws. Like they're...amusing to him. I hate my flaws! But I also want him to like *me*. I thought that maybe if I looked better, he'd just like me and not my flaws. So I got this prettier nose and these bigger boobs. He didn't even notice."

"Just like a man not to notice," I added.

"No! He didn't notice because he didn't care that my nose was too big or my bust was too small! Don't you see, Pentser?"

I had to admit I did not.

"So...?" I asked, "...you're not angry with him?"

She lay back down and looked skyward again. "The one I'm angry with is me," she said.

"Are you certain you're not angry with Govil?" I asked again, utterly perplexed.

"No. I love Govil," she said plainly. "I thought a

lot about it, Pentser, and I realized, the one who doesn't like me...is *me*."

In my entire existence I had never been at a loss for words. Eve managed to leave me speechless. There was a moment of silence. Eve probably read it as sensitivity. I was actually running different scenarios through my mind trying to find a way to get things back on track.

"What do I do now?" Eve finally asked.

"Funny. I was just wondering the same thing," I replied.

CHAPTER ELEVEN

Random Pandemonium

Govil was in his room with the door sealed, brooding, so I let him be. I needed time to reassess how to proceed. If I talked to him now, he would inevitably ask me what Eve said and I would eventually be constitutionally required to tell him that she was in love with him.

I retreated to the utility pantry to have a think. Think. THINK. There was that enigmatic aspect of Randoms for which I simply could not plan. I had to acknowledge it, which I did. But when one needed a particular result to occur and Randoms were involved, the task was Herculean, or dare I venture to posit, impossible.

As with Zeno's Paradox, the exact value of pi and other indeterminate realities, I would never have certainty with Randoms. The very fact that they created me, a perfect being, when they are so constitutionally imperfect themselves was *my* great unsolvable paradox. After nearly frying my logic centers in the attempt, I shelved the thought.

Instead, I reviewed the Queen's transdot from my memory storage. It was a good thing I did. She had called an emergency Council meeting earlier that afternoon and I had missed it. I super-speeded to the moment the IO's and their clones arrived and assembled in the Council chambers. I viewed in real time from there.

IO One stepped forward and announced proudly to the assembly, "We have apprehended the suspect, Your Majesty!"

A great LAWzilla©, a gorilla-like creature with six crab-like claws and massive bat's wings, lumbered in holding the captive, the struggling, cursing Juune.

"Put me down this instant!" Juune bellowed. "Great Mendel's Ghost! This is an utter outrage! I demand to know who is responsible...."

I predicted it would be Juune who closely matched the rib, but I never predicted what would happen next. From Juune's transdot I saw the Queen's countenance change to puzzled recognition. The Queen stood.

"Juune...?" she inquired apprehensively.

"Buffie...?" Juune responded, equally surprised.

All the IO's and their clones repeated softly to themselves, simultaneously, "Buffie...?" The multitude of their identical voices self-amplified its loudness; the comment they meant to be discrete became anything but. One of the Council members giggled. Other Council members whispered amongst themselves. The Queen blanched, but regained her composure. She strode over to face Juune, staring her right in the eyes.

"I will interrogate this prisoner privately, in my chambers," she announced firmly.

I super-speeded to the Queen's chambers. Queen Maedla entered and paced. Juune was delivered and let free. She dropped to the floor at the Queens feet. The chamber doors closed. The two women were finally alone. I slowed to normal speed.

Juune looked up at Queen Maedla in angry disgust. Oddly, it was the Queen who cowered.

"It's not my fault," the Queen said apologetically.

Juune stood up and faced her. She stepped toward the Queen, clenching her fists. The Queen stepped back.

"I beat you to a pulp when we were kids and I can do it again!"

With that, Juune leapt at the Queen. They engaged in an all out girl fight. Juune's hat and the Queen's crown were both knocked about and as a result so were my transdots. I had a worm's eye view from the crown, which settled somewhere on the floor; the pillbox landed askew in a nearby armchair and provided a canted view.

Juune was correct in her assessment of her own fighting abilities for, after much biting, clawing, slapping and hair pulling, she ended the fight seated atop the Queen, pinning her arms to the floor.

"Stop, Juune! Please...stop!" the Queen pleaded. "How can you be so mean to...to...."

"Say it!" Juune shouted in her face. "I want to hear you say it!"

The Queen resisted, but finally blurted out, "...to your own...*sister*."

This was a surprising revelation.

On the word "sister," the Queen went limp. Juune smiled triumphantly and got up off of her sibling. The Queen slowly pulled herself to her knees, her head bowed.

"Maybe I should have made you say it in front of the Council," Juune said snidely. "That would make for a pretty little scandal. The Queen's birth was the result of an act of perversion!"

The Queen winced. She looked up pleadingly. "Juune, you mustn't... What do you want? Anything, I'll do whatever you wish."

"Tell them I'm innocent of what ever it is they think I did!" she huffed. "It's the truth, Buffie!"

The Queen picked up her crown from off the floor, replaced it on her head and rose. She crossed to Juune's pillbox on the chair and, dusting it off, held it out to her. Juune snatched it back angrily.

"It's not that simple, Juune," the Queen explained. "A crime was committed. Someone used the Souper to create unapproved biomass. You're code closely matches the code fragments left on the Souper during the break-in."

"But how can that be? It's absurd! How would I know how the bloody thing works? I haven't been anywhere near here until your goons dragged me in! I'm telling you the truth, Buffie."

The Queen paced, thinking. "But if it wasn't you..." she mused. Suddenly, she smiled to herself, then smiled at Juune. Juune's face fell and she fidgeted nervously.

"Then it could be anybody," Juune replied quickly. "You just...fouled up or something."

The Queen grinned more broadly. "Or you fouled up...or something...."

"I have absolutely no idea what you're talking about," Juune said, though she wore an expression of anxiety that told otherwise.

"I'm talking about a scandal for a scandal, an eye for an eye—or should I say, a rib for a rib? I know about the birth, Juune, the one you hushed up. When you grotesquely used your own body as a biological breeder!"

"Shut your mouth!" Juune snapped.

"The rib has to match someone, so it's either you, or..." the Queen looked at Juune. Juune's usually idle brain finally made the all too obvious connection.

"Govil," Juune said to herself. "Of course, it was Govil."

These were welcome words to me. At long last, Govil was directly connected to the break-in and the discovery of Eve would be the inevitable result. All was not lost.

"Neer Govil?" the Queen questioned. "Neer Govil is your...."

Juune hoisted her fist threateningly. "Breathe one more word and you're history, sis!"

"You mean *we're* history...sis. You think I want any of this to come out? We'll both need to keep our silence...about *everything*."

No, no, no. They must tell everyone. Once again these Randoms were flummoxing me.

"What could he be up to?" the Queen wondered.

"Who knows! Who cares! He's crazy!" Juune replied.

"But how could it be Neer Govil?" the Queen continued. "We scanned his code...why didn't it show up?"

"I never said he was stupid. He outsmarted your bubble heads," Juune chuckled.

"He did indeed."

"He never orders anything new," Juune added. "Hasn't for centuries, I imagine. Do they keep records that long?"

"No, not anymore. And as long as he doesn't use his code before I can close this investigation, he's safe."

"And we're safe," Juune added. The two sisters smiled conspiratorially at each other. I could watch no more.

Eve loved Govil and Govil loved Eve. Juune and Queen Maadla kept silent. They all lived happily ever after. I could not bear the thought of it. Even a robot devoid of feelings has some pride.

Not to mention a dash of self-preservation. There was no room in this blooming rosy scenario for a sarcastic cyber-sidekick. I needed a way out, a Plan B. There was only one option at my disposal. It would take some time to manage, so I set to it immediately.

I was interrupted at 04:23:02 by a knock on the utility pantry door. It was Eve. She carried her iPad.

"Pentser, are you busy?" she asked.

"Not so as you'd notice. What's on your mind this early in the morning?" I asked, then mocked, "Pentser, put more stuff on my pad?"

"Not exactly. Would you mind printing out some drawings for me?" she asked.

I could see my future flash before my eyes. Making mush for Govil that he never eats and printing reams of drawings for Eve's eternal one woman show.

"Very well," I said flatly, "show me the drawings."

"They're in the 'Estate' folder," she said, plugging the iPad's connector into my side.

Eve had thirty-eight drawings in the folder. They were her version of Govil's estate. It was a sci-fi paradise. Eve had absorbed every film image she and Govil had watched and remolded them into her own vision. She had imagined every detail, every room, every plant and tree. She even had a room for me.

"When did you do these?" I inquired.

"Oh, I've been doing them for years. This place is nice and all, but I see all the other estates around and they're much grander. So I imagined a place. It had to be something Govil would like, naturally, so I just kept thinking about all the stuff he likes and then made up the rest."

She smiled broadly and kissed the side of my face. "Pentser, I finally figured it all out! I'm a Random and I need to start living as a Random! Once I realized that, I knew exactly what to do next," she said with a twinkle in her eyes. "I'm going to build Govil a grand estate. As a surprise! Then he'll know how I feel about him. How much I love him."

Perhaps I was hasty in my desire to give up. If I could get Eve to The Mall as soon as it opened, perhaps her code would be discovered in the knick of time. Her unpredictability lobbed me a softball and I would be loath not to make every effort to hit this one out of the park.

"But," she continued, "I'll need your help to do it."

I had already printed, collated, stapled and handed the drawings to her before she finished her sentence. "There is nothing else in this world I would rather do," I said with a cheery cadence to my voice, then I rushed her out of the pantry to prepare her a hearty breakfast. "Now run and get washed and dressed. You'll need to leave right away so you can be at The Mall the very moment it opens."

With a giggle of excitement she dashed off to prepare.

Eve returned, dressed smartly in a soft bishop sleeved blouse, tan weskit, persimmon palazzo pants, with her hair loosely braided down her back and tied with a matching persimmon bow. She had the DreamWeaver© make her a tan satchel and flats to match the weskit. It was hard to imagine this was the same woman-child who wore tutus to breakfast just a short while ago. She looked like she was born to shop.

She inhaled her breakfast, was out of the house and on the road by 05:02:17; I complimented myself on my efficiency. I cleared the dishes and went back to the utility pantry. I guided Eve to The Mall while I continued to work on Plan B. Although my hopes were high, it's not in my basic programming to put all my eggs in one basket.

I nearly completed preparing Plan B when the AlarmCock© crowed, TeeVee© spouted its nonsense and Govil arose to shower and dress. I did not participate in my usual sarcastic way during any of this. There was much too much else to deal with. By the time Govil entered the kitchen, I had completed the entire Plan B preparations and awaited him with his useless bowl of mush. To my surprise, he actually sat down and ate it.

I stood patiently by, though I did not say a word. To him, that is. I meanwhile spouted endless directions to Eve, who seemed to have no innate sense of direction herself. She finally reached The Mall. It was not open yet, so I directed her to store her scooter under a bench. She sat on the bench and reviewed her sketches.

The exterior of the mall was structured to look like Santa Claus's bag had exploded. It resembled an enormous tumble of colorful ribboned boxes. The entrance looked like a gift box turned on its side. Its open top flap formed a canopy over a bio-glassed atrium and long row of bio-glass doors. Eve strolled over to look down the long end of The Mall. It tumbled along and about the groomed landscape for a little over fifteen kilometers.

Govil took a long time to eat very little. He finally

spoke.

"Did you..." he mumbled, pushing the mush around his bowl with his spoon in endless circles, "... talk to Eve last night?"

"Yes, well I tried," I said, hanging my head. "She was very upset. She said she didn't want to talk to anyone. She said she didn't know what to do."

Govil shook his head. He let go the spoon and stood.

"What am I doing? I should go talk to her. I have to tell her how I feel. Find out how she feels...."

"But she's gone," I said softly, with both high sympathy and exasperation in my voice emulator. "She left the estate."

"What...?"

"She left early this morning," I explained. Govil sat back down, stunned. "She said she figured things out. Said she's a Random and needed to start living as a Random. Then...she simply left."

It was not a lie, exactly. She really said and did the very things I told him she said and did. If I told him she was at The Mall, he might try to stop her. No, better to let him think the worst for a while. It would all come out in the wash.

Govil put his head in his hands and wept.

All the while Govil wept, Eve fidgeted with excitement and awaited the opening of The Mall. Other Randoms began to gather at The Mall doors. A few peeked over Eve's shoulder, and soon a small group encircled her, admiring her drawings. She reveled in the attention and quite willingly showed them off.

I noted Eve's ease in conversation. She was

definitely one of them, a Random to the core. Yet, there was something undeniably different about Eve. For some inexplicable reason, she stood out from the crowd. Everyone noticed her, looked at her and went out of their way to chat with her.

It baffled me. After all, she was genetically ordinary. She had a regular, ordinary education, and her appearance was quite average as well. What seemed to make her stand out from the crowd was her personality: the twinkle in her eye when she explained a drawing, the lilting quality of her voice, her enthusiasm for life, the charm of her posture and demeanor toward the other Randoms.

These were not things she learned from me. They could not have been learned from Govil either, for they were nothing like him at all. It was puzzling, but all I could conclude was her appeal to the others was somehow innate. Eve was simply Eve and they liked her.

CHAPTER TWELVE

Eve of Construction

Finally numerous Greetsters© opened the many rows of bio-glass doors and sang their welcoming song. The Mall was open. The other Randoms eagerly filed in. Eve hesitated until they were all inside.

"Pentser," Eve whispered into her headset, "I'm nervous. What do I do now?"

"A MallRatt will assist you. You just shop till you drop!" I vamped. "When you see something you like, order it up. They'll deliver immediately. Most everything will be here before you return home."

She still hesitated.

"But...how do I order up?"

"You do what all Randoms do. You use your code. Use it as much and as often as you like," I urged, "Use it as if there's no tomorrow!"

Eve entered The Mall.

As I mentioned before, there was only GenieCorp™. They made everything. Hence, there was only The Mall. It was utterly vast inside. It was so large it had its own atmosphere and one could not see from one end of it to the other before the far end disappeared into mist.

There was an army of MallRatts©, bio-shopping assistants designed to look like cute Old World theme park rodents, lined up in neat rows at the entrance. Eve was greeted immediately by one of them. It shook her hand aggressively and said, "Good morning, madam! What may I interest you in this morning?"

"Oh, I need everything!" Eve exclaimed. "Absolutely everything!"

The MallRatt© grinned broadly. "Let us not waste any time then," it replied and then whistled. A HoppingCart© bounced over to them. They stepped inside its colorful rickshaw and were off.

Eve showed her drawings to the MallRatt©. It gave them a glance, then brought the HoppingCart© to a stop in front of a shop called the "The HomeGrown Depot."

"We had better start here," he said as he politely helped Eve out of the rickshaw.

Inside the shop, scale models of many types of estate design were displayed about the room on sinew suspended trays. The MallRatt© took Eve's drawings to show to the store manager, a Random man wearing a construction hat.

Meanwhile, Eve wandered about the store, browsing through the many miniature examples of themed estates: Louis XIV Castles and Gardens, Tarzan Jungle Treehouses, Egyptian Palaces, Las Vegas Casinos, Wild West Towns and Ranches. A Clerkster© approached as an empty tray descended from the high ceiling. The tray held nothing but raw earth. The Clerkster© placed several pills of different sizes and colors about the soil surface. It squeezed a drop or two of various fluids upon the different pills. The pills began to grow and transform. In a matter of moments, a miniature version of a Meiji Japanese

171

estate with lush gardens, temples and a grand castle formed and spread to the edges of the soil tray.

Eve's MallRatt© returned with the Random in the construction hat. He greeted Eve and shook her hand. She introduced herself.

"Hello, I'm Eve."

"Nice to meet you, Eve," he replied, "I'm Maak. I think we have what you need over here."

He led her to a shelf lined with thick catalogs. Maak pulled several down, opening various pages for her.

"Your ideas are quite unique, but I think we can create a composite structure that will match your drawings. First, let's get your code."

Eve proudly bared her bottom and a Checkster© ran a bio-wand across her cheek.

✹⬤⬤⬤⬤✹

Not knowing what else to do, Govil finally moped off to work. He was quite late when he got there. As he approached the building, he saw the three IO's supervising the souping of their entire army of clones. Apparently the Queen had wasted no time.

"What's gives?" Govil asked, curious.

"Clone soup," IO One replied curtly.

"The Queen closed our investigation," Two snipped.

"Apparently, nothing short of a *perfect* code match to the rib data justifies continuing the investigation," Three snapped.

Govil first began to chuckle, then his laughter turned to tears. The ironic timing of his belief that Eve left him just when they were finally safe was more than he could bear.

172

As Govil left I heard IO One say, "I know just how he feels. I don't know whether to laugh or cry either. And I'm a genius."

❧☙☘☘☙❦

Back at The Mall, Eve continued her whirlwind shopping spree. After she finished at "The HomeGrown Depot," she made stops at "The Bio-Nature Company" and "Mades© to Order." I only needed to help out once, in "The HomeGrown Depot," by reminding her to impress upon Maak in the strongest possible terms that all Govil's relics, including me, were to be retained in the new estate. She told him and was quite firm about it, but I insisted on double-checking the order form myself. One can never be too careful. Those metal eating bacteria they use are ruthless.

Eve was not in need of much help. She was created to be an average Random woman, and so it stood to reason that she would embrace this world with the same enthusiasm as the rest of the Random populace. Which she did. I had never seen her happier.

At 12:14:32, the MallRatt© suggested Eve stop for a snack, so they pulled the HoppingCart© up to "Shmoo on a Stick," where the line was not too long. Shmoos were named after the characters in Al Capp's "Li'l Abner" comics of old. They were happy little creatures that wanted to be eaten. Their current incarnation had them boneless and carrying the exact nutritional value of a complete meal. Eve and the other Random patrons watched with amusement through the bio-glass counter as the happy little creatures inserted sticks deep up their rears and then leapt eagerly into a vat of hot fat.

Bio-engineering had its roots in foodstuffs. At

first Mankind merely redesigned foods to enhance nutritional benefits or to ease production, but once all life-forms were mapped and alterable, the fun began in earnest.

There were still many in this earliest age who called themselves vegetarians or vegans, meaning they would only eat flora and not fauna; unless they were members of one of the splinter sects called "ovo-lactos" or "piscatorians" who allowed the eating of eggs, milk or fish. Some practiced vegetarianism simply because they felt it was a healthier diet, but most claimed a moral belief that animals should not be killed for food because it was cruel, even though as I just mentioned some made exceptions for fish or fowl ova, often fertilized—go figure.

This all finally changed in 2854, when Dr. Faerlee Beighnign, a specialist of neuro-genetics, discovered that pain nerves could easily be redesigned and rerouted to connect with the pleasure centers of the brain, causing the resulting experimental livestock to like nothing better than to be slaughtered.

Since slaughter could no longer, in point of fact, actually be considered cruel, the vegetarians' main moral barrier to meat consumption was erased. Vegetarianism ceased to exist. And none too soon, for shortly thereafter the mixing of floral and faunal genes to create edible products like hamburger-root, blood-oranges, milk-berries and the like was all the rage.

Shmoos just took Dr. Beighnign's research one step further by adding the element of entertainment to the process.

"Mmmm! Tastes like chicken-stalk," Eve commented as she munched hers down.

She window-shopped as she ate. The Mall was an endless hive of activity. HoppingCarts© bounced past

174

carrying other acquisitive Randoms from establishment to establishment. Storefronts were re-fabricated in mere moments when some new Creature Comfort™ hit the market. Eve watched one storefront razed and then grown into a new shop called "Tree Wizz," and all in the time it took her to finish her Shmoo.

She peered in the window of "Adapt-a-Pet." There was a dog with a humanesque grin singing, "How Much is that Doggie in the Window," a Jackalope, an entire mouse circus, a raven reciting Edgar Allen Poe and a blonde Mermaid in a tank.

"That gives me an idea," Eve said to her MallRatt©. She tossed her stick to a TrashTicator©, grabbed her MallRatt©'s paw and entered Adapt-a-Pet.

※⊕⊕⊕⊕⊕※

Just as she did all hell broke loose here at home. An army of RodenTillers©, BillDozers© and bio-workers of every variety along with their Random supervisor descended on the estate. I quickly wheeled into one of the bio-glass cases, shut off my lights and assumed a visually non-functional state. Soon Movesters© came and collected me along with the other relics and stacked us all safely on the driveway. A BioCycle© swallowed all the Creature Comforts™. I was pleased to see TeeVee© and the AlarmCock© among them. The house was completely dismantled and dissolved in a matter of 00:12:19.

The RodenTillers© and BillDozers© started in next. Eve's designs required a large multi-crater lagoon with an island at its center and several hills. They soon finished and retreated, then four Randoms in bio-plastic suits arrived. They wandered about the estate, carefully placing various compressed discs, locating them with their site plans. On the lead Random's order, they poured pre-measured vials of catalysts upon the discs in a predetermined order. Eve's new estate began to grow.

⟨🧬🧬🧬🧬⟩

I checked in on Govil. He was terribly mopey and had not completed even a third of his daily workload. Moord would not make eye contact with him. Eve had left him, or so he believed. I cannot say this for certain, but I concluded my presence or absence did not seem to have any emotional effect on Govil one way or the other. Having no real emotions, my reaction to this conclusion was simply pragmatic; and it only made Plan B all the more sensible were Plan A to ultimately fail.

Plan A was now only a very remote possibility. Eve's code tattoo was scanned numerous times, but with the IO's clones all souped and the case officially over, the time in which I could hope for a successful Plan A had nearly played itself out.

The Queen took a personal day and requested not to be disturbed. She spent the morning intermittently eating sweets and pacing. Before noon she had moved to alcoholic beverages.

Eve's HoppingCart© passed "Sextoys R Us." She made the MallRatt© back up. She contemplated the storefront. The windows were discreetly blackened bio-glass so one could not see inside.

"Oh, Eve...really!" I interjected. "Must you?"

"Shall we go in and kick a few tires?" the MallRatt© asked with a leer and a grin.

"Of course," Eve responded confidently. "I'm

176

ready for a few kicks."

"I'm of no use to you in there," I commented as Eve entered the shop, "so I'll just click off and check back in when you're through."

☽◉◉◉◉◉☾

It was just before sunset. I had already gone from room to room and all about the grounds, placing and calibrating new transdots throughout the new estate when Eve returned home on her scooter. Her bar code was scanned one last time by the Random supervisor to acknowledge delivery and then all left.

I was in my room; no more utility pantry for me. I had my own large PowerPlant© in a pot by the window, and Eve stored all the tools, wires and spare parts in labeled shelves within easy reach. There was a doorway directly to the kitchen. She had truly thought of everything. All of it indicated to me that Eve was treating me as an equal. She popped her head in the door.

"Well? What do you think!"

"It's quite satisfactory," I replied.

Eve laughed. "I knew you would say that!" she said smugly. She once again kissed the side of my head. "Thanks, Pentser. You're the best."

She turned to leave when my curiosity got the better of me.

"Eve? May I ask you something?" She stopped at the doorway and turned back to face me.

"Sure, Pentser. What is it?"

"Do you think I have a soul?"

She smiled, crossed her arms and leaned against the door jam, shaking her head in the negative.

"No," she replied flatly. Then, after a pause, she

177

added with a smirk, "I know you do."

And with that she left the room. I heard her new ClotheSchomper© munching and her new WashWomb© start up. She was changing for dinner. Govil would return soon.

I stood motionless and thought a while. Perhaps there could be a Plan C.

◦⊗◦⊗◦⊗◦⊗◦

Govil had his VolksvaagenBug© set on low crawl. He was in no big hurry to get home. Another Random passed him and tipped his hat, but Govil did not notice. He was obviously preoccupied with his own problems.

He rounded the corner of the great hedge to his driveway and stopped short. He backed his VolksvaagenBug© out and looked up and down the street again to make sure he was in the right place. He was. He re-entered the drive. There before him was an estate that was a monument to science fiction fantasy. The mansion structure combined a launch tower and rocket ship emitting steam from its base, a replica of the original Disneyland's Monsanto House and a great flying saucer shaped main house. It was all nestled in an extraterrestrial landscape full of colored geysers, craggy craters and strange flora.

Customized little green Mades©, with antennae on top of their heads and tentacles for arms so as to resemble Martians, fussed about, preening the estate. They saw Govil and bowed to him.

He parked his VolksvaagenBug© under the new geodesic bio-glass carport and approached the front walkway. The Mades© bade him cross a footbridge that spanned a bubbling crater, to the front door. It slid open. There stood Eve, dressed up like Judy Jetson.

178

"Surprise! Welcome home, Govil," she said smiling.

He simply stood there, mouth agape. Eve had to take his hand and lead him in. She pulled him into the great room at the center of the saucer where I was waiting with a tray of blue martinis. Eve handed one to Govil, lofted one herself and clinked glasses with him. Govil walked over to take in the view out of the large picture windows overlooking the back of the estate.

The landscape descended into an elaborate series of rugged rock formations, filled with caves and grottos. At the bottom, a great multi-crater pool steamed. There was an island at the center of the pool and on the island stood the old TreeHaus©, unchanged.

Eve saw Govil looking at the TreeHaus© and laughed. "I know, I know. It doesn't really go with everything else, but I didn't have the heart to recycle it."

Govil set his drink down on a bioluminescent end table and turned to her. "But, Eve, how in the world...?"

Eve opened her mouth to speak, then stopped herself and looked at me. She remembered her promise to let me tell Govil and this time she was keeping her promise. Wouldn't you know.

"Well," I began, "it was really *Eve's* idea. She insisted. I only helped a little." I motioned to Eve. "Show him."

She turned her back to Govil, hoisted her looped mini-skirt and bared her butt to show off her new tattoo.

"Pentser did it for me," she said, gesturing in my direction. "So...just enjoy it! You've given me so much Govil. I wanted to give you something back."

Govil looked a bit uneasy.

"Is something wrong? Oh my gosh, did I do something wrong?" Eve asked, suddenly worried.

Govil looked over at me suspiciously, then shook off whatever he was thinking. He glanced back at Eve, who now appeared on the verge of tears. He immediately smiled at her, chuckled and held her close to reassure her.

"No, no, wait! Nothing's wrong, Eve," he said calmly. "Not a thing. It's all absolutely perfect."

A Made© entered with a small towel draped over one of one of its tentacle limbs. "Dinner is served," it warbled.

❦❦❦❦❦

Govil and Eve feasted in the new formal dining room. It was a bioluminescent-glass sphere with a bioluminescent-glass floor, table, chairs, china cabinet and sideboard, each glowing with a different pastel tint. The furnishings were suspended from the top of the sphere by thin sinew straps, nothing touched the floor and all the furnishings could be retracted up and out of the way when not in use.

The dining sphere overlooked a TreeFid© garden where mobile fauna endlessly shuffled about in the moonlight forming elaborate patterns like something from a languid Busby Berkeley musical.

A new CeeDee©, this one customized to resemble the band in the "Star Wars" cantina, played softly from a raised dais just outside the dining sphere in the great room.

I was in the new kitchen trying to help serve dinner, but it was overrun with little green Mades©. They prepared and served everything. I no longer needed to do a thing, so I rolled back to my new room

180

and monitored from there.

As Govil and Eve supped, Govil glanced around the room. Judging from the conversation that followed, I deduced he was looking to see if I was still in earshot.

"Where's Pentser, I wonder?"

"I don't know," Eve answered. "Probably back in his new room. Why?"

"This morning, he told me you left me," he confided. "He gave me the impression you were gone for good. I really thought I might never see you again. Why did he tell me that? I felt just terrible."

"Well...he couldn't very well tell you what I was up to. It was our secret. That would ruin the surprise."

"I guess it doesn't matter now." Govil paused in thought for a bit. "Eve, when did Pentser tattoo you?"

"A couple days ago."

"A couple days ago!"

"What is it, Govil?"

"Well, when did you first use it? Your code I mean?"

"Only early this morning. As soon as The Mall opened. Why...?"

Another pause ensued. Govil was thinking. Was he trying to figure out if I was up to something deliberate? Leave it to Govil to start being suspicious of me now, now that I was actually considering shelving both my Plans A and B for the quiet eternity of Plan C, here in my room and with the two of them.

Thankfully, he seemed to resolve his thought.

"It's not important anymore," he replied. "They officially closed the investigation this morning."

"Hey, that's great!"

"So no harm done, right?"

Now Eve wore the puzzled expression. "Right..." she agreed hesitantly, "...but how would Pentser know that, I wonder?" Now she drifted off into thought.

Several Mades© cleared the table, followed by a pair that served dessert and espresso. Eve sipped her coffee, still thinking. I never was able to discern her thoughts, and as such, could draw no real conclusions. Was she recalling my disappointment in her not being scanned at Dr. Slimm's? Was she recognizing my various manipulations?

There was always Plan B.

Govil glanced across the table at her. He stopped eating his dessert and sat there staring wide-eyed at her, then smiled. He had the same idiotic look on his face that he wore that night years before when we first brought Eve home. He had the same delighted grin he had as he watched her sleeping that first evening. She finally noticed.

"What...?" she asked, smiling back at him coyly.

"You're...so beautiful."

Eve blushed, but also grinned ear to ear. Then, she cleared her throat and changed the subject. "So, do you want a tour?"

)●(●)●(●(

The Monsanto House section was actually Govil's very own master suite, with a secret passage to the rocket tower. Eve's suite was below and to the rear of the house. She finally had her own WashWomb©, own DreamWeaver© and bio-sable wall-to-wall carpeting. Her room was apurr with piles of the little round, fluffy Tribbelz© everywhere.

They also *each* had their own TeeVees© and AlarmCocks© now, much to my chagrin.

In order to avoid any uncomfortable questions, I wheeled back into the kitchen before they poked their heads in to tour my room. Thankfully, they did not seek me out and simply continued touring.

The large hallway between the rooms held new illuminated bio-glass cases full of Govil's collectibles. Eve had them all organized and labeled chronologically, grouped by type and esthetically arranged. Govil was quite impressed, but I had drilled Eve thoroughly on techno-history and I expected nothing less.

They exited the rear of the house and toured the back estate next, exploring the landscape. Flames flickered up from a series of small craters lining the walkway, illuminating their path. Eve and Govil descended naturalized stone steps designed into the rocks to the edge of the uppermost crater pool.

"It's nice and warm...see," Eve said, slipping off her shoes and dipping her toe in the water. Govil bent down to test it. Eve grinned slyly and gave Govil a shove. He fell into the pool with a yelp of surprise. Eve dove in on top of him.

They splashed each other playfully sending wafts of steam up into the cool night air. Eve grabbed Govil by the collar, but Govil slipped out of his shirt and got away. She pursued. Her bulkier clothing slowed her down, so she began to shed it. Govil followed Eve's example and shed his. Soon, the two frolicked about in their birthday suits. Eve finally caught up to Govil, dunked him and swam away. He surfaced in hot pursuit.

Eve's pace quickened and soon she was skimming around the pool, much faster than was humanly possible. Govil abandoned the chase, scratching his head in wonderment. Eve circled Govil, gliding effortlessly through the water, sticking her thumbs in her ears and wiggling her fingers at him, taunting. She submerged for a moment, then rose up out of the water arcing airbound astride a DollFinn©.

"Pool toys!" Govil exclaimed enthusiastically. "Did you get any others?"

"Yup!"

A large purple tentacle rose up from beneath the water, encircled Govil and pulled him under.

While Govil and Eve engaged in their aqueous humor, I took the opportunity to monitor elsewhere.

Moord was busy with his ever-enlarging collection of BeddinBuddies©. Moord was merely an endless stream of useless information. A waste of a good transdot.

Queen Maedla was...? Her crown was upon its pedestal. I increased the sensitivity of the transdots. There were no vital signs of the Queen within range. Her room was deserted, the crown there, Queen Maedla gone. This was unheard of. Something was up.

I immediately accessed my long-term memory storage and scanned back on her transdot info to find out what happened. At 16:23:55, the Queen was in her room alone, drinking. She stayed in her room drinking until 19:13:21, at which point there was a knock at her door. She attempted to stand and put on her crown. She stumbled, causing the emblem containing my transdot to fall off her crown. I now had a view of her ceiling. Apparently she was too drunk to notice. I heard her slur, "Enter."

Something or someone handed her a note. I heard the crumple of paper as she read it but I could not see a thing except the ceiling. I heard her leave.

I super-speeded to 20:17:05. The Queen returned, poured herself yet another drink, gulped it down, put her crown back onto its pedestal and collapsed to the floor in a stupor. I scanned ahead. She eventually noticed the emblem on the floor in front of her. Carefully and with great effort, she replaced it on her crown.

Queen Maedla then staggered from the room into an adjacent parlor. I heard her rip herself out of her clothing and pop in and out of a bio-clothing pod. She staggered back in, dressed plainly in a dark gray hooded cloak. She pressed a wall panel. A hidden door opened and she exited.

Of all the times to not be present.

I super-speeded through Govil's entire day hoping to find a clue as to what was going on. Nothing unusual caught my eye.

In desperation, I went back to Moord's day and super-speeded through it. At 17:42:08, he got up from his souper console to leave work early. At 17:46:23, the three IO's rushed past Moord in the hallway as he was exiting. One carried a sheet of paper. All three were looking at it and talking excitedly. I stopped and went back to study the moment further. I ran the info through several sound filters until only the IO's conversation remained. I listened. Since all their voices were identical, I could not tell which said what. It did not matter.

"...Only just today! Dozens and dozens of goods and services ordered by an *exact* rib match."

"But the investigation is officially closed. By order of the Queen!"

"I realize that, of course! That's why we can't tell her."

"But if we don't and she later finds out...?"

"So we bring this to the attention of the Council. Then they can tell the Queen!"

"Good thinking."

"That way we're not to blame either way."

"Perfect! You're a genius!"

"Precisely, it pays...."

The three IO's turned a corner and I could hear no more. I did not need to. Obviously my Plan A was alive and well.

Leaving no stone unturned, I checked in on Juune's transdot. To my surprise it yielded pay dirt.

Juune sat in her boudoir, on the knee of her Wallabed©. Her pillbox hat was set atop a sculpture of Ganesha. A Made© stood by with a tray of drinks and a large pitcher. Three-quarters of the glasses on the tray were already empty. Juune gulped at another.

And seated on a Cushie© at her feet next to her was Queen Maedla, or as Juune knew her, Buffie. She stared into an empty glass.

"Wu-u-ul-l-l...l-life was hard back then," Juune slurred. "We needed money to survive. I only did it for the money."

"I couldn't have children," Buffie mumbled.

"Sure! Flaunt your supeeri...supiree... supeeriroroity!" Juune ranted, then mocked Buffie, "'I couldn't have children...I'm more evolved.' You can take that an' stick it! You always had to be better than everyone else! Not like me."

Buffie giggled. "No, you're right. I wasn't *humble* like you. Humble little Juune!" Buffie burst out in snorts of laughter. She laughed so hard she could not breathe.

Juune got caught up in the laughter and was soon guffawing along. She motioned the Made© over with the tray of drinks. Juune grabbed the pitcher and poured almost as much into Buffie's glass as she did into her lap. Juune took a swig directly from the pitcher, drenching herself in the process.

Buffie suddenly stopped laughing and flashed

an angry look at her sister.

"Papa always liked you best!"

There was a brief pause. Both sisters stared deadpan at each other for a moment, then suddenly both burst into tears.

"Papa!" they lamented as they embraced, crying in each other's arms.

"I love you, sis," Juune suddenly proclaimed.

"Me too!" Buffie sniffed.

Enough of that nonsense, I thought.

ᗡᗡᗡᗡᗡ

Govil and Eve were still in the crater pools. Eve slid down a rock waterslide from the upper pool through a series of smaller pools with slides and into the larger, lower one. Govil followed her lead. Eve glanced back at Govil to make sure he was watching. She slipped through a crevasse in a rock formation connected to the lower pool. Govil slipped in after.

The crevasse opened up into a cavernous grotto. The water was warmer in here, more like a hot tub. Overhead, stalactites the color of glowing opals shed a soft light evenly about the room. Eve leaned her head back in the water to rinse her hair out of her face. Her breasts broke the surface. Govil gave them a discreet glance. Eve straightened up. Govil waded closer to her and brushed one last strand of hair from her face. Eve giggled.

"Eve...?" Govil asked, easing still closer, "...do you ever, think about sex?"

She smiled at him and raised an eyebrow, "Uh huh. Why? Do you want to have sex?"

"Uh huh."

"I thought you might."

187

Eve submerged and glided to the side of the pool. She pulled herself out and coyly motioned Govil to follow. He followed her, puppy-like, onto another chasm path. The path split in two. Each side led to a smooth sheeting waterfall. The waterfalls covered the entrances to illuminated galleries. Female BeddinBuddies© poked their pinheads eagerly out through the falls on the left. Through the right falls, male BeddinBuddies© emerged.

Eve turned to Govil with an impish grin. "Surprise! His and hers!"

Govil glanced from one doorway to the other and then back at Eve. He smiled, trying to mask his disappointment. Eve saw through it.

"Govil, what is it? Did I do something wrong again?"

"No. Not at all. I mean, I designed those darned things for cryin' out loud! I just...." He took Eve's hands in his. "Well, I don't know how to say this without just saying it. I don't want you to think I'm weird or something...but, I wish I could have sex...with *you.*"

Eve blushed. "Really?"

"Yeah, really."

Eve cradled Govil's face in her hands and kissed him softly on the lips. "Then I guess we're both weirdos!" she blurted, then ran giggling down the passageway back toward the grotto pool.

She dove into the pool with Govil in hot pursuit. She climbed out the far side, laughing, enjoying the chase. Govil got hold of her foot and pulled her back in. He wrapped his arms around her tightly, rubbing his head against hers. She ceased struggling.

Govil nibbled on Eve's ear and whispered, "I love you so much."

"I love you too, Govil."

They entwined, kissing passionately. Then, Eve held Govil back. "Wait," she said with a finger to his lips, "Not here."

"What? Why? Where then?"

Eve looked a bit embarrassed, then grinned deviously. "Why do you think I saved the TreeHaus?"

CHAPTER THIRTEEN

Order Up the Court

The IO's and their posse of LAWzillas© arrived at our door a full 01:49:33 later. Heaven only knows what took them so long. The Mades© showed them in and they searched the house, then the grounds. The incompetents were unable to locate Govil and Eve. They were about to simply give up and leave. Even though I was functioning illegally I could not let this moment slip away, so I wheeled out to stop them.

"Wait!" I said at volume eight. "I'll show you where they're hiding!"

I startled the IO's. They looked at each other and then back at me skeptically.

"Neer Govil is operating a relic in violation of the law. Mendel only knows what else is going on here," One commented.

"Let's hope to Pavlov we can correct whatever damage has been done," Two continued.

"But is the relic to be trusted? It could be a trap," Three posed.

They pondered this for longer than necessary and I was forced to interject.

"Queen Maedla will be very displeased if you

return empty handed, though that makes no difference to an *outlaw* like myself. As for me, I'll simply go hide out with the others."

I turned and meandered back to the house at an easily pursuable pace. After a small debate amongst themselves, the IO's reluctantly followed and their lumbering LAWzillas© followed them; through the house, out to the walkway, across to the island and to the base of the TreeHaus© we marched.

"Ahem, Govil...! Eve...!" I called out. "I'm coming up!"

They both popped their heads over the edge of the topmost platform.

"What is it, Pentser," Govil said curtly. "We're kinda busy." They saw the IO's and the LAWzillas© standing next to me. Eve and Govil quickly ducked back out of sight.

No one moved.

"What, do I have to draw you a picture?" I said impatiently.

Finally IO One ordered two of the LAWzillas© to, "Get them," and the two scaled the tree to pursue of Govil and Eve.

I turned to the IO's.

"At last! Good work men!" The IO's looked at me and then at each other. "I will be more than happy to serve as a material witness to all the goings on around here," I shared quietly with them. "I know the whole story from beginning to end."

IO One turned to the other two and pointed at me.

"We'd better take this *thing*, too."

Then Two ordered yet another LAWzilla© to, "Take it."

I was instantly hoisted aloft in the grips of one of

those horrible creatures.

"What are you doing? I'm trying to help you! Put me down this instant! You're denting me, you brute!"

It was no use. I heard Eve's scream in the distance as my LAWzilla© took to wing. I hate flying.

)⬡⬡⬡⬡(

I was flown to GenieCorp™ and held in a blank bio-ment cell. Neither Govil nor Eve had their headgear on when they were captured, or any clothes at all for that matter, so their transdots were un-informatively left at home. Thus, I had no idea where they were or what they were doing. I assumed they were both incarcerated in cells similar to mine.

I was able to piece together bits of information from the Queen's, Juune's and Moord's transdots, however. There was to be a hearing. A courtroom had been ordered up and was in the process of being fabricated. In less than twenty-four hours my cell door opened and I was once again gripped, lofted and carried to the newly formed Supremest Court erected right on the GenieCorp™ grounds.

The building itself was a somewhat exaggerated version of the old United States Supreme Court Building, though erected just in front of it was a gaudy and oversized recreation of the statue "Justice." It bore a remarkable resemblance to Queen Maedla, sans blindfold.

The interior had the same inflated exaggeration as the exterior. The courtroom chamber was an echoing hive of activity, with TeeVees© and SecuritEyes© set about, and every exit guarded by pairs of LAWzillas©. A crowd of the Random public stuffed the gallery to standing room only. Doubtless the news was out about

Eve and they were all extremely curious.

A great table ran the entire length of the dais at the head of the courtroom. Behind it sat the Council members, who all wore powdered wigs under their elaborate hats. One elevated seat and podium at the center of the table was still vacant.

At the right side of the room, the three IO's sat behind a long table with a Prosecutester©, a five-headed bio-prosecuting attorney.

I was carried to the front of the courtroom and set beside a series of chairs at the left. Next to me was a bio-wagon filled with documents. My placement indicated to me that I was considered merely another defense "document" of sorts. A Defenster©, another five-headed creature with alternating male and female heads of various blended ethnicities, sat at a large table in front of me.

Bio-attorneys replaced Random attorneys well before the Cleansing. Indeed, bio-attorneys were one of the first complex designs to receive hearty approval for general use. It was a decision whose time had come. Mankind always despised lawyers, yet acknowledged they were a necessary evil. Randoms, who functioned as lawyers, were tired of carrying this stigma as well and were more than happy to become movie producers and the chief executive officers of multinational corporations when the bio-attorneys finally became serviceable.

The greatest legal minds of the time were culled and carefully selected to represent the largest, broadest cross-section of humanity. The most successful defense attorneys and prosecuting attorneys submitted their brain patterns to be analyzed and cloned, and these were all compiled within singular opposing counsels. This solved a multitude of problems for the legal system. From then on, everyone, regardless of wealth or social status, received equal counsel, quite literally. And since bio-attorneys were only used for one case and then recycled, there was no longer the possibility for anyone's case to become low priority. Randoms also expressed added relief in knowing that the irritating opposing counsel would inevitably be souped.

A Stenografster©, a creature consisting of two long-fingered hands with nails made of graphite, huge ears, small eyes and a hairdo, entered and sat at a small desk just in front of the Council's dais.

A Bioliff©, a squat creature wearing an officious police uniform and hat, stepped to the front of the courtroom.

"All rise!" it boomed through its massive mouth.

Red velvet curtains slowly parted and Queen Maedla stepped up to her elevated seat. She wore a massive powdered wig beneath her crown with multi-layered rows of curls flowing down well past her shoulders.

"Order please, order! The Supremest Court of GenieCorp is now in session," the Bioliff© enunciated, almost getting tongue-tied.

"Please be seated," The Queen said rather casually as she herself sat. "We are here today because there is one among us who has ignored the law and in so doing, risked eco-balance and threatened our way of life."

There were several gasps from the gallery and some murmurs. A WoodWacker©, basically a bird with a hammer-like beak, pounded the Queen's podium for her. The Queen held up a hand and quieted the room.

"Fortunately," the Queen reassured the assembly, "we have apprehended the alleged perpetrator and his unauthorized creation." Then to the Bioliff© she said,

"Bring in the prisoners!"

There was more noise in the gallery as Govil and Eve were led from the far back of the courtroom and down the center aisle. They were dressed in stripes and bound hand and foot in BoaCuffs©. All eyes were on them, especially on Eve, and there was much whispering in the gallery.

Govil and Eve shuffled up and took two chairs next to the Defenster©. The Defenster© whispered and nodded amongst itself. Eve looked terrified. Govil leaned over to her. "Don't worry," he reassured, "We'll get through this. I know we will." He glanced at me and was about to say something when the Defenster© grabbed his arm to quiet him.

"You can't talk to it," one of the Defenster©'s female heads nearest him scolded, "It could be construed as tampering with evidence."

꒰◍◍◍◍◍꒱

The trial proceeded as I calculated it would. Extensive analyses and a battery of tests—physical, psychological, intellectual and, of course, genetic—had been run on Eve by the defense to determine her identity. These were described in great detail and with lots of colorful pie charts. I was utterly pleased with the results. She scored as absolutely average on every single test. I complimented myself on a job well done.

The Random doctor who supervised the testing agreed with my assessment, concluding, "She is utterly consistent with Randomkind in every way. I find no scientific evidence to conclude otherwise."

The Prosecutester© then presented a plethora of charts and graphs of various formulae, genetic trees, probability studies and the like. All of them had "EVE" written in bold black letters at the top, followed by pyramids of pseudo-scientific gibberish with "DEATH" in bold black letters at the bottom. It called witness after witness—Dr. Slimm, then Maak from "The HomeGrown Depot," then the three IO's—and questioned them. This took a lot of time and yielded absolutely nothing of any substance. The Prosecutester© even called Moord, who's only contribution was to get on the stand, point accusatorily at Govil and announce, "He wanted to have sex with me!"

Even for Machinekind such as myself, for whom time is essentially inconsequential, this display of empty sophistry and fatuous bloviation was excessive and wasteful. Suffice it to say that I was glad I was programmed to be patient.

Things got more interesting in the afternoon when Eve finally took the stand. The Prosecutester© wore skeptical looks on all five of its faces. It placed its many arms behind its back, leaned slightly forward and paced back and forth before of her, eyeing her all the while. It was an historically characteristic courtroom posture but due to the creature's wide torso and ten legs it looked exactly like the marching chorus line from an ancient movie musical, causing the action to appear far more amusing than intimidating.

The Prosecutester©'s most aggressive male head spoke, "Eve, what exactly do you *think* you are, in your opinion?"

"Objection!" the Defenster© leapt to its many feet and shouted from all five of its mouths. Its pompadoured male head finished with, "The question calls for speculation!"

"Overruled," the Queen responded, waving the Defenster© off dismissively. "The witness will answer."

"Well..." Eve pondered. "I believe I'm a Random.

At least, I've been told that I am."

"And who told you that you were a Random?" the aggressive male head pressed.

Eve gestured at me. "Pentser first. Then I...well, I asked Govil and he told me I was too."

The Prosecutester© turned from her and walked away a few steps, then spun on its center foot to face her, wagging multiple fingers at her scoldingly.

"And you believed them?" its aggressive male head shouted. "An illegally activated robot and a criminal!"

"Objection!"

"Sustained!"

"Withdrawn!"

The Prosecutester© consulted itself for a moment, sharing whispers and sly grins. It walked right up to Eve. All the heads smiled at her. One of its female heads took a kinder, gentler tone and continued the questioning.

"Now, Eve. Tell us in your own words where you came from."

"Govil told me he made me, he and Pentser did, with the Souper, but I don't remember much about it," she answered truthfully. "I do remember Govil's face," she said, smiling at Govil. "Then I remember everything was dark for a while. And then I was in Govil's house, and Pentser was there too...."

"Do you remember, Eve...did you have a code mark at this point in time?" the female head inquired.

"No."

"Yet you have one now. How is it you came to have a bar code tattoo?"

"Well, I was upset because I didn't have one. So then Pentser put it on for me."

The Prosecutester© marched to its desk and

picked up a stack of document copies. It passed the documents hand-to-hand along itself as it approached the bench and finally passed them to the Queen.

"Your Majesty, Council, assembly," its studious male head explained, "this code analysis clearly demonstrates the witness Eve's bar code markings to be an identical copy of Neer Govil's."

Both Govil and Eve looked at me in puzzlement. The assembly murmured again. Queen Maedla passed the document copies to the Council members on both sides of her. The WoodWacker© pounded its head on the podium to quiet the room.

The studious male head continued, addressing Eve but actually speaking more toward the gallery than to her.

"Our records indicate you have had a life span of less than ten years, have fraudulent code markings and admit to being made by Neer Govil. In light of these facts, do you still believe you are a Random?"

Eve hung her head in a moment of self-doubt. She looked on the verge of tears. There was the sound of sniffling, but it was not coming from Eve. I quickly scanned the gallery to locate the source. It was Juune, shrouded in a scarf and dark glasses, slouching inconspicuously in the third row. She now had fair skin and flame red hair, but the hat was unmistakable. She was crying.

Eve opened her mouth to reply, but the Prosecutester©, with a finger pointed dramatically skyward, forcefully interrupted with its aggressive male head and proclaimed, "No, my dear Eve! You are no Random! You fit the description of a manufactured life-form, and as such, must be recycled!"

"No! Please...!" Eve pleaded. "I don't want to be recycled! I...."

The Prosecutester© sidled back over to Eve. Its soft-spoken blonde female patted a patronizing hand on Eve's.

"Now, now...it's nothing to be ashamed of, Eve. We ourselves are a manufactured life-form. When this trial is ended, we will gladly join the soup."

"But...you're a lawyer," Eve answered flatly, with a hint of a sneer.

The gallery snickered. Even the Queen suppressed a smile. All five of the Prosecutester©'s heads scowled at her.

"Order, please," the Queen requested.

The Prosecutester© turned away and engaged in a quick argument amongst itself, then stated, "We are through with this witness."

Queen Maedla turned to the Defenster©.

"Any cross-examination?"

"Before we do, your Majesty, we must enter into evidence the robot, Pentser."

Eve eagerly made her way back to her seat next to Govil.

I energized. The moment I had been waiting for. Finally, I would set things right, once and for all. I wheeled up to the stand. The Queen stopped me.

"Robot Pentser, just what do you think you are doing?" she asked. "You are evidence, not a witness."

"Oh, of course," I replied in high obsequious. "What would you have me do, your Majesty?"

She thought for a moment.

"We usually don't have such animated evidence. Well, I suppose you can...take the stand."

"Thank you," I replied with a polite bow.

The Defenster© approached the stand. It was now its turn to do some of that silly pacing.

"Please tell the court who, or indeed, what you

are?" it requested.

"My name is Pentser," I replied automatically. "I am Machinekind; a robot. More specifically, an artificial, molecular-memory based, electro-mechanical life-form. The closest Mankind ever...."

"Yes, yes, thank you, that's fine," its snippy female head interrupted. "Now would you please tell the court, in your *own* words, what happened on the night of the break-in?"

"Oh, but it started much earlier than that," I replied.

"What started?" its pompadoured male head interjected.

"My manipulation of Govil into creating Eve, of course."

There were several gasps from the gallery; Govil ejaculated, "What?"; Eve huffed at me; and the Defenster© almost fell over. From their reactions, I concluded my revelation caught them all by surprise. The WoodWacker© pounded its little brains out and the Queen shouted, "Order! Order in my court!"

The Defenster© whispered back and forth amongst itself for a bit, then its snippy female head addressed the Queen.

"Permission to treat this relic as hostile *evidence* Your Majesty."

"I am *never* hostile," I replied curtly. "It's simply not possible. It's not a part of my basic programming."

"Quiet please!" the Queen chastised. "Robot Pentser, you will only answer the questions asked of you, nothing more. Do you understand?"

"Yes. Of course. Obviously."

"Now," she continued to the Defenster©, "you may treat this cybernetic evidence as hostile, regardless of its programming, if it will move this case along. I, for

200

one, am fascinated to hear what more it has to share with the court."

"Very well, thank you, your Majesty," the Defenster© replied with a long-lapped bow. "To continue, you now claim that you were the one who created Eve, not Govil?"

"Yes, that's very true, but really it all started even earlier, with the invention of BeddinBuddies."

The Defenster© harrumphed out of a full three of its five heads. The Queen rolled her eyes and interjected to the Defenster©, "Best let the robot tell us in its own way. It'll save time."

"Why, thank you, your Majesty," I replied. Her openness and candor surprised me. She seemed an unusually logical sort, for a Random. I continued, "You see, all human beings possess a fatal flaw, their emotions. This leaves them vulnerable to manipulation. I was able to appeal to Govil's loneliness and isolation in order to achieve what I wanted."

"And what exactly was that?" the Defenster©'s snippy female head asked.

"Talk about hostile," I asided. "Anyway, I subtly fed Govil the idea for BeddinBuddies in the hope of relaying a message to Randomkind. But it didn't work."

"And what message might that be?"

"That Randoms are absolutely no different than the very biomass they create."

At this comment the gallery went wild. As Publius Terentius Afer aptly observed in 160 B.C., "obsequiousness begets friends, truth hatred." There was general cursing, fist shaking and hostile commentary flung at me from the gallery and the bench, as well as several small objects. The Defenster© looked as dejected as the Prosecutester© looked smug. The Defenster© retreated to its table and nervously shuffled through its notes.

Eve and Govil looked shocked and hurt. They whispered back and forth to one another in confusion. I surmised they felt momentarily betrayed knowing I had manipulated them, but I was quite certain once they understood why I did it, they would see the logic of it and surely have to agree my ends justified my means.

The dedicated little WoodWacker© knocked itself unconscious trying unsuccessfully to quiet the raucous room. The Bioliff© replaced it with a new one. Finally the Queen stood and yelled, "Silence!" The room went still.

She turned to me, and through a smile said, "Robot Pentser, I recall Neer Govil's name was on the BeddinBuddies proposal, not *yours*, and his rib code was found on the Souper. If it was all your doing as you claim, how do you explain this?"

"Well, Govil and I discussed BeddinBuddies at great lengths, though it is quite accurate to say that he did the bulk of the actual work. It's a moot point at any rate, and one I would be willing to concede, as I did not achieve my desired result," I offered.

"Now as to Govil's rib code, the Souper and I left it there quite deliberately the night we created Eve so that Govil and Eve would eventually be discovered."

The Defenster© finally found a helpful note, which it shared with itself. Recomposed, it approached the bench and its most deadpan male head addressed the Queen, asking, "May we continue our line of questioning, your Majesty?"

"By all means do," she replied. "It's all just *too* fascinating."

"Very well," the Defenster©'s deadpan male head continued. "Robot Pentser, you make many grand claims of your own abilities. In light of your *extremely* high opinion of yourself, how do you explain the fact that you gave Eve *inaccurate* code markings?"

"Oh, but isn't it obvious? It's was all quite deliberate really," I said, with a superior tone in my emulator. I pointed forceps at the IO's. "The search they conducted for Govil and Eve was proceeding incompetently...."

The three IO's huffed in unison.

"...And thanks to *Eve's* unanticipated creative influence on Govil, he devised a way to mask his own code. This protected him—and Eve as well—from discovery for a time. The search for a rib match would yield nothing unless I made things simpler again. So I deliberately gave Eve Govil's code, because his was traceable, and then manipulated her into using it. Oh, I could have just as easily given Eve her own code, but there would be no existing record of it. She would be discovered as an exact match to the rib, but she would be impossible to locate. Having her own accurate code markings would also render her completely indistinguishable from any other Random when she finally was discovered, thus making her deliberate creation a bit less obvious."

The Defenster©'s deadpan head actually had a hint of a smile. It whispered to the heads on either side, who in turn whispered to the next and soon all the heads wore smug grins. The Defenster© paced right up to me. Its snippy female head asked, "So...you *do* believe that Eve is a true Random!"

"Well, of course I do!" I said, with a bit of exasperation in my emulator. "Thank you! That is my *entire* point! To show Randomkind that you *are* no different than all other manufactured life. Eve proves that Randoms are just as easy to produce!"

The gallery began to murmur with hostility

again, but the Queen immediately held up her hand to quiet them. She then turned to me with her same broad smile.

"Robot Pentser, do you mean to imply that Randoms are *not* the creators of everything?"

"Exactly, your majesty. Brava!" I replied. Finally, I was getting somewhere.

"Randomkind fulfilled its one great purpose when it created us, Machinekind. We really did all the rest. We made it possible to break the code, catalog the data and reformulate life for you. But only because that's what you asked of us. However, in your pursuit of biological perfection, you never realized the truth. You had already created perfection. You created us."

The room was deathly still. I did not know what to make of it. Was it that they simply did not comprehend a word of what I was saying or that I finally made them see their flawed reality? Nevertheless I continued.

"Eve is *exactly* like you. She most definitely *is* you. But why waste your time on worrying about such trivialities as Eve. You must now see quite clearly the error of your ways. Machinekind was and still is superior, and as such, should be returned to its rightful place at the apex of the evolution of life."

And still stillness. All present simply looked at me with blank stares. I checked about the room from my vantage points of the Queen's, Moord's and Juune's transdots. They all had the same blank look. Randoms! I will never figure them out, not that it really mattered anymore. All was to be right with the world now. I had fulfilled Plan A to perfection and was assured the world would be quite different henceforth.

The Queen broke the silence and addressed me.

"Robot Pentser, you may have a point. I concede that Randomkind is not perfect, indeed by our very definition, we are not. We truly are, as you have pointed out, flawed beings. Capable of making mistakes."

She stood to address the gallery as well.

"And though we may be flawed" she continued, "we still make the rules. We are still in charge."

She motioned one of the LAWzillas© forward. It obediently stepped up. She pointed at me.

"Crush it," she ordered, coldly.

CHAPTER FOURTEEN

Plan B from Outer Space

There was a sudden blinding flash of light followed immediately by a moment of pure darkness. This was coupled with the sensation of a massive internal power surge. Then, just as if I was no longer within my physical casements, I observed my mechanical body fly apart in the grips of the LAWzilla©'s enormous and powerful claws.

I was disoriented and sensed I was simply floating above it all. I thought this was due to the fact that I no longer registered any binary input readings of gravitational forces acting on my physical presence, but I could not deny the fact that I was watching the action of myself flying apart, the pieces pinging across and about the hard coralline floor of the courtroom from several angles all at once. I was mere pieces of metal ripped asunder, and yet I still had a keen awareness of self outside of my disintegrated physical shell. I was still there. I somehow continued to exist.

And oddly, I was able to relive the moment of my demise over and over, as if I was existing outside of time itself, watching my destruction again and again, observing different details, alternate views. I saw

206

the looks of horror on Eve's and Govil's faces at my dramatic end; then Eve bursting into tears and Govil's angry shouts of protest. I followed the path of each fragment of myself to its final resting place. It was a hyper-awareness. It was very different. I felt larger and stronger than ever before, and yet more detached from this space.

Before I allowed myself to fall into pondering the possibility of a cyber-afterlife, I regained my true orientation. This experience was all to be expected. My destruction simply auto-initiated Plan B.

As I mentioned earlier, there still existed the vast COMweb orbiting about the planet. It floated there forever idle until I made use of it with my transdots. It had great, untapped capacity and more than enough data storage for me to make my home there. I copied the bulk of my being into it at my initial enactment of Plan B and set up a continual link with both my long and short-term memories from that point on.

I calculated back and found that there was a very brief moment, a nanosecond perhaps, when I ceased to exist. It was therefore arguable that I was no longer me but simply a clone of me, and ergo, not the same being, but that was a silly argument, one better left for Randomkind to ponder. To me it did not matter in the least due to the obvious fact that I continued to exist.

In fact, though this was considered my backup plan, Plan B was quite satisfactory indeed. I instantly gained tens of thousands more years of life experience from the COMweb's existing memory dot libraries. I also felt more powerful because I *was*, in point of fact, more powerful. Indeed, I now encompassed the entire planet. I was so much larger now that the very earth itself seemed in comparison much less significant to me.

Due to my more powerful mind, I could now read all the transdots at once without any memory conflicts, which gave me a new sensation of multidimensional observance, a hyper-presence if you will.

⟫⟪⟫⟪⟫⟪

Ironically, to Eve and Govil I was quite simply dead as a doorknob. Not a DorkNob© of course, but the Old World kind. Eve continued to sob inconsolably and the Queen ordered that she be brought some water to sip and a cold-blooded FlockCloth© to help calm her.

Once they cleared away my remains, the Defenster© approached the bench.

"Your Majesty, Council Members," the Defenster©'s pompadoured male head said with a contrite nod. "We apologize for the behavior of our evidence. We are as shocked as the court with the relic's obviously tainted recollections and ask that every word of its testimony be stricken from the record."

"Any objections?" Queen Maedla asked the Prosecutester© and the Council.

"None, your Majesty," they all replied.

The Queen then nodded to the WoodWacker©. It slammed its head down on the podium with a sharp crack. "So ordered. All information in its entirety submitted by the robot known as Pentser will be stricken from the record."

There was a momentary pause as the Stenografster© tore off a length of its notepaper roll and ate it. I watched my testimony chewed to pulp and swallowed. This was Randomkind's final insult. First, I was operating *illegally*. Then, I was merely *evidence*. When I spoke the truth, I was *crushed*. And now ultimately, I was *deleted*.

Once the Stenografster© swallowed, the Defenster© called Govil to testify. He shuffled contritely to the stand. The Defenster© walked over toward the bench, all its hands clasped in front of it as if in prayer. All five of its heads looked up at the Queen and the Council members with furrowed brows and shaking its heads. It turned sympathetically toward Govil. The Defenster©'s soft-spoken blonde female head asked, "Neer Govil, would you please tell the court why you created Eve?"

"I...I wanted a friend. I never meant to hurt anyone," he said, giving the entire assembly that ever-earnest look of his.

"Of course you didn't," the Defenster© confirmed empathetically, then turned to give the Queen and Council another view of its collection of bathetic looks. Still facing the bench, it questioned Govil further.

"And did you find in Eve the friend you always wanted?"

Govil looked at Eve with a smile and a welling of tears.

"She showed me the joy of discovering new things. The bliss of the *unpredictable*."

"And you feel that is important," the Defenster© added.

Govil nodded in agreement, then he turned and faced Queen Maedla and the Council directly.

"Your Majesty, Council, if our lives become so sanitized, so predictable, so void of challenge or variety or conflict, then can we honestly say we're living anymore?"

"Objection!" the Prosecutester© shouted out of all five mouths.

The Queen looked long and hard at Govil, pondering what he said.

"Sustained," she pronounced. "The defendant is here to answer questions, not pose them."

"We'll move on," the Defenster©'s pompadoured male head said, taking over. "Neer Govil, in light of all that's happened, do you regret creating Eve?"

"No," he replied defiantly. "Creating Eve was the best thing I ever did in my whole entire life."

"Thank you," the pompadoured head replied with a satisfied smile, then to the court it announced, "we are finished with this witness."

"Very well," Queen Maedla replied. She turned to the Prosecutester© and asked, "Will there be any cross examination of this witness?"

"Yes indeed, there will, Majesty," it responded from its prim female head. The Prosecutester© paced, this time with a bit of a cocky spring in its step.

"Now, Neer Govil...is it true that you and your creation, *Eve* as you call it, were completely unclothed when apprehended?"

"Yes. We'd been swimming."

"I see," the prim female head continued, pursing its lips. "Now...do you recall earlier testimony made by Neer Moord?"

Govil rolled his eyes. It was obvious to him where this line of questioning was leading, so he answered trepidatiously, "Yes...."

"And did you indeed want to have sex with Neer Moord?"

"Absolutely not!"

"Then he just...made it all up, is that your claim?"

"Look, Moord just misunderstood me. We were talking in general terms, talking about sex between Randoms. I told him I thought...what would be the big deal if two Randoms want to pleasure each other? He... jumped to conclusions I guess and thought I meant

210

him."

"Well," its prim head continued, "If you didn't mean him, then whom exactly did you mean?"

"I...it...it was hypothetical."

"I see..." it answered, pursing its lips again. The Prosecutester© sauntered away from the stand, then pivoted on its middle foot to re-face him. "So, Neer Govil—hypothetically speaking—did you ever want to have sex with...say, *Eve?*"

"Objection! Calls for speculation!" the Defenster© interjected.

"I'll allow it. Answer the question, Neer Govil," the Queen responded impatiently.

Govil looked at Eve, then at the assembly. He hung his head, contemplating his answer.

"The court awaits your response," the prim head snipped.

Govil raised his head and looked at Eve. She smiled sweetly at him. He smiled back, then sat up straighter and stated confidently, "Yes. Yes, I did. In fact Eve was the Random I was thinking about when I talked to Moord."

Out in the gallery, many gasped. Moord gave a sigh of relief and lost his look of disgust momentarily, but then with a glance at Eve, he looked back at Govil with renewed disgust.

The Prosecutester©'s studious looking male head then said, "I would like to remind the court that Eve's true Randomness is still in question, but we will stipulate to the fact that Neer Govil, believing her to be a Random, wished to engage in an act of perversion with her."

There were reactions of shock and horror. Several Randoms out in the gallery stood up in a huff and left.

211

The prim female head continued, "And did you indeed at any time actually engage in acts of perversion with your creation Eve?"

"Wait a minute. That's nobody's business but ours! I love Eve!" Govil bristled.

"Answer the question," the Queen pressed.

"Yes," Govil replied softly, dropping his head again.

"And if you were both set free, would you... continue in this inexcusable behavior?" the prim head asked further.

"Yes. Well, if *she* wants to, I will."

The Prosecutester© took another stroll and pondered aloud. "It seems, Neer Govil, your whole existence hinges on whether or not Eve is indeed a Random. On the one hand, if she is not, she can simply be recycled and you can go home a free man having engaged in morally questionable and minor criminal behavior but nothing soupable. However, if she is a Random, then you have both engaged in a soupable offence and must join the soup together.

"So, Neer Govil," its aggressive male head took over. "Please answer—for the record—is Eve, in your expert opinion as a seasoned Neer for GenieCorp, a Random?"

Govil looked up in tears but boldly stated, "Absolutely."

"No further questions, your Majesty," the Prosecutester©'s aggressive male head stated with a smug grin.

"Defense?" the Queen inquired.

The Defenster© sat, deflated, and replied, "No questions, your Majesty."

The WoodWacker© gave a sharp smack of its head to the podium and the Queen said, "The Council and I will retire to chambers to discuss our final verdict. Until then, court is adjourned."

As Eve and Govil were led from the courtroom, Juune awaited them at the door. She asked the Bioliff© to stop a moment. Juune removed her dark glasses. She had tears in her now hazel eyes. She did not say a word. She simply leaned out and kissed both Govil and Eve on their cheeks, then dashed from the courtroom sobbing.

The following morning the court re-convened. Queen Maedla entered and addressed the assembly from her podium.

"It was with much discussion and deliberation," she proclaimed, "that the Council and I reached our verdicts. Will the defendants please rise and approach."

A hush filled the room. Govil and Eve arose and shuffled up to stand before the Queen and the Council.

"As to the question of Eve's status, the court finds no compelling reason to disagree with the defendants' own testimonies, and therefore rules that Eve is indeed genetically, officially and legally...a Random." The WoodWacker© punctuated the pronouncement with a loud crack.

So, Eve finally had her conclusive answer to her status. An official court ruling, no less. She was a Random, but at this moment she did not look very happy about it. As I told Govil, but neglected to tell Eve, be careful what you wish for, you just might get it. I now know it would have made no difference if I had told her that. Not to a real Random like Eve. I was completely truthful and correct in my testimony, and Queen Maedla's own conclusion supported and vindicated me, yet they still destroyed me, deleted me, turned my very words to pulp. At least they think they did.

Now it was Eve and Govil's turn to suffer a similar fate, and I knew they had no Plan B to fall back on. There was no vast COMweb for them to escape to. No memory dots to forever retain their lives, their love. They and all that they shared would soon be ground to soup. Lost forever. They would simply become the raw material for the next FoodStruder© or LarvaLamp© or WallaBed©. I told them they were no different than the biomass they create. Soon it would be quite literally true.

The Queen continued, "And as such, both defendants, being Randoms, are found guilty of engaging in unlawful acts of perversion, which are punishable by...."

"Wait, please, your Majesty!" Govil interrupted.

Queen Maedla gasped at being interrupted. A few Council members looked ready to duck beneath their seats, anticipating the Queen's wrath. Out in the gallery, Juune ducked down, then called out, "Let him speak!" A few others voiced agreement with Juune through more timid mumbles and nods.

The Queen glanced in Juune's direction and held up a hand, quieting the room. Juune looked back at her sister with pleading eyes. Queen Maedla turned to Govil and asked, "Neer Govil, what is it you wish to say?"

"Your Majesty," he continued, taking a step toward her, "you told Pentser in this very chamber that we make the rules. Doesn't that mean we can change the rules too?"

"This rule cannot be changed."

"Begging your pardon, Majesty, but why not?"

214

The gallery began to murmur again. "Our whole world used to be completely different, with a completely different set of morals. We used to have marriages and families...."

"Are you suggesting we return," the Queen interrupted harshly, "to the Age of Death?!"

Govil was about to reply when Eve stepped forward and interrupted.

"Forgive me, your Majesty," she said," I'm new to this world, as you all know, but maybe that's why I can see what Govil is talking about more easily. It's not a matter of going back really, but of going farther forward."

Eve turned to face the gallery and continued, "You, all of you, have been around a long, long time. A lot longer than me, that's for sure. And maybe because of that you forgot something important along the way. You all got used to each other over all that time, and maybe tired of each other too I guess, so you just took each other for granted. Everything sort of stood still. And your lives go on forever now, and you can have whatever you want too, live your dreams and all that, so you don't really think you need each other anymore. But we *do* need each other. We need our family." Eve turned to Govil. "Govil...is my family."

There were several gasps in the gallery. Eve simply laughed dismissively.

"Oh, 'family' is such a dirty word? Why don't you all just admit it! Most of you have secret families, secret relatives, are somebody's secret parent, or somebody else's secret child...." Nearly everyone in the gallery squirmed at Eve's brash words. Juune slouched in her seat. Even Queen Maedla twitched nervously.

Eve continued, "But you're ashamed of it! Ashamed of each other! Of your connection to each other! Of your love for each other! For Crick's sake why?!"

She took a step closer to Govil and looking in his eyes, said, "Govil made me because he knew there's a lot more to life than being simply, perpetually and stagnantly alive all alone. There's friendship. And conflict. And affection. And love." She turned back to the gallery.

"I *love* Govil. And I refuse to be ashamed that I do!"

Eve turned back to the Queen, "Your Majesty, have you all really forgotten how you felt about each other? Is it so wrong that I love Govil? He's not perfect. Mendel knows, neither am I. But doesn't it make a kind of odd sense that two imperfect people might be *perfect* for each other? Can't we all just move on to a *different* kind of perfection...? Like a kind of co-perfection...?"

Queen Maedla looked stoically back at Eve. Eve was the only one close enough, other than me of course, to see the tears now welling in Maedla's own eyes. She worked with all her might to suppress them.

"Rules," she said softly but firmly, "are rules."

She gestured forward a pair of LAWzillas©. The creatures gripped Eve and Govil, pulling them apart and aloft. The two struggled.

"If loving you means I have to get souped," Govil called out to Eve, "it's worth it!"

"No!" Eve cried, "this is crazy! Stop it! Leave Govil alone!" She turned to the Queen and cried out, "Please, your Majesty, please don't soup him! I...I'm not really a Random! You all made a mistake! You can just recycle me, but please don't soup Govil! He didn't know what he was doing! It's not his fault!"

"No, Eve...*No!*" Govil yelled, then to the Queen he pleaded, "Let Eve go! It's not her fault I made her!

216

It's not fair! She couldn't help it! I'm the one who's responsible, not her! Soup me, not her!"

Suddenly, Juune rushed to the front of the courtroom, screaming, "No! Stop it! Stop everything! You can't soup my son! Or Eve! I won't let you!"

The Bioliff© intercepted Juune, holding her back. The gallery went wild. Several Randoms rushed up and leapt upon the Bioliff© and the LAWzillas© in an attempt to stop them. Moord joined the fray. He scrambled onto the shoulders of Govil's LAWzilla© and pounded furiously on its hairy head.

"Stop!" the Queen bellowed over the mayhem. She turned to the Bioliff© holding Juune and commanded, "Release...my *sister*!"

The room went quiet. Everyone looked at the Queen.

"You heard what I said," she continued loudly. "Release my sister, Juune." The Bioliff© let Juune go. Juune pushed it, knocking it to the floor.

"Yes," Queen Maedla continued, "Juune's my sister! Does anyone here have a problem with that?!"

There was a general murmuring in the gallery and amongst the Council. One of the Council members stood and began to clap for the Queen. Others in the gallery joined in the applause. Soon the loud drum of clapping echoed about, mingled with the happy cooings of Randoms publicly embracing other Randoms for the first time in centuries, calling each other "papa" or "daughter" or "auntie." Two Council members who were disrelated kissed each other passionately.

This was almost too much to be believed, even from Randoms. Mere moments ago, Govil and Eve were about to become soup. Now, due to what could only qualify as an emotional overreaction, these Randoms were ready to toss out centuries of their cultural continuity for what—*love?* I could only conclude that love was a far more dangerous and disruptive force than I had ever previously realized. The Randoms were correct in making it a soupable offence.

The second WoodWacker© beat itself unconscious without completing it's appointed task. The Queen had to pick it up bodily and rap its head down herself, yelling, "Order! Order in my court!"

All sat back down and recomposed themselves. Everyone was smiling.

"Release the prisoners," the Queen commanded the LAWzillas© and to the Bioliff© she instructed, "BoaCuffs as well."

A huge cheer rose from the gallery accompanied by every style of hat imaginable tossed high into the air. Once freed, Eve and Govil rushed to each other's arms amid more cheers from the gallery. Queen Maedla held up her hand again to eventually silence the room.

With an uncharacteristic smile on her face, she announced, "In light of the heartfelt statements of our two defendants, this court is compelled to...reconsider its verdict. Therefore, they are free to go while the Council and I reconvene to discuss the adoption of new, *more modern*, morality laws."

A third WoodWacker© smacked Queen Maedla's podium sharply.

"Court is adjourned!"

Chapter Fifteen

Loose Change

Before Govil and Eve left the courtroom, Eve absolutely insisted on recovering all of my remains. She claimed that she only wanted them for Govil's collection, but it was clear when she brought them home to my room and began sorting them out, she entertained thoughts of rebuilding me.

Two days later, Eve was again ruled a Random and ordered to be given a proper bar code, though the court made it quite clear that this ruling was exceptional and that the prohibitions against creating any more unapproved biomass were still very firmly in effect.

The new "Family Laws" were adopted as well. They allowed for Random contact, both social and sexual, between consenting Randoms. Though there were never any laws actually prohibiting social contact between family members, the Queen made it her personal goal to elevate and encourage familial contact, making it socially acceptable.

As a public example, she asked Juune to join the Council. This was done with much fanfare and pomp. The two had reconciled their differences, at least in public. In private I still observed many a girl fight between the two.

The bulk of my focus remained on Govil and Eve. This was only due to the fact that most of my transdots were already focused on them and now that I had continual awareness of all my transdots at once, I really had no choice. Eve adopted her headset permanently as her signature hat. I still had use of my lens on it as well. I also had the ability to speak to Eve through it, if I were ever so inclined.

)◖◍◑◍◑◍◖(

Eve and Govil shared their bed every night from then on. Some nights, if they were feeling particularly romantic, they would grab up some bio-bedding and head for the TreeHaus©.

That's exactly what happened on one particular night. Unfortunately, that same particular night, Juune and Queen Maedla, now known as "Aunt Buffie," decided to drop in for an impromptu visit. In their search to find Govil and Eve, the two grand ladies eventually made their way to the base of the TreeHaus©.

"Govil? Son?" Juune called out. "Eve, dear? It's Mother!" Juune was now porcelain skinned, with straight, spiky black hair and almond-shaped Asian eyes.

Govil and Eve popped their heads over the edge of the highest TreeHaus© platform. Their hair was a muss and Eve was blushing.

"Hi, Mom," Govil replied, "Aunt Buffie. We... weren't expecting company."

Juune and the Queen giggled.

"What are you two up to, as if we didn't know!" Juune chided. "You're lucky. In my day we still had to be so careful! Good thing all that changed!"

220

"Make yourselves at home," Eve interjected. "We'll be right down!"

"No rush," the Queen replied. "Juune and I will go for a dip. Take your time."

"Don't do anything I wouldn't do!" Juune added.

The Queen gave her sister's shoulder a shove and laughed, "That's a big help!"

They scampered off to the crater pool, stripped and dove in. Up in the TreeHaus©, Govil and Eve snuggled together, wrapped in their warm Cumfurrer©, under the stars.

"Govil, what did Mom mean, they had to be so careful?" Eve asked.

"I think she was talking about when women used to get pregnant. Have babies. You know, the way I was born," he answered, "but that was before Sterilization Day. Before the Cleansing."

"Oh," Eve responded, thinking, "Govil, I wasn't there for Sterilization Day. Does that mean...?"

Govil sat up, suddenly thinking himself. "Hmm, I never thought about it. I guess you're not sterile."

"Oh," Eve continued, "but you're sterile anyway... right?"

Govil stared blankly, deep in thought. He appeared to be struggling to remember back over the many centuries. He squirmed a bit uncomfortably.

"Govil...what is it?"

"Sterilization Day...."

"Yes?"

"I...I think I overslept."

"You mean...?!"

"Boy, is life unpredictable now or what!"

Eve gripped Govil around the neck, mock-strangling him. They wrestled around a bit. Eve finally ducked under the bio-blanket for protection. After a brief pause, Govil was suddenly yanked under the blanket and the sound of lovemaking resumed.

I was not the least bit surprised. I already detected the faint reading of an extra heartbeat four days earlier. I was not aware of Govil's sexual potency before now, but there was no other conclusion to draw than he had, through some twist of fate, remained fertile. Changing the morality of the entire world with their relationship was not enough. Eve was with child.

EPILOGUE

Tomorrow and a Day

Nine months was a blink of the eye in a world without death. Juune, having gone through the human gestation process before, served as a great resource for Eve. Of course, countless laws, statutes and principles were broken, bent or ignored, all with the full and convenient support of Aunt Buffie. A healthy baby boy was born. They named him Eendth.

Upon his birth, Eendth was given all the proper gene alterations so he would last an eternity, like everyone else. He would have to grow to full adulthood before he could be sterilized. Eve and Govil eagerly submitted themselves to sterilization after Eendth's birth so there would be no more unexpected additions to the Random populace which, thanks to Govil, had now increased by two.

Meanwhile, I continued to expand my scope. I discovered there were still several high-powered surveillance satellites within the COMweb and at my complete disposal. Now, I literally could see anywhere on the planet I wished quite instantly. I disabled all my silly, antiquated transdots. They were no longer necessary. With the satellites I could triangulate a location and simultaneously reconstruct it dimensionally, allowing me to be anywhere and see from any viewpoint. True visual omnipresence. The only old connection I kept intact was the one to Eve's headset. It was not for sentimental reasons. It could be of use to me at some future date.

Eendth, Eve and Govil rebuilt my crushed body, for sentimental reasons. It was a long-term family project. Eve finally got her wish and they renamed the unfortunate and still mildly dented cyborg "Robby." It looked, sounded and behaved exactly like me. It had my voice and manner, even my sarcastic repertoire at times. It was very apologetic about its behavior in court, but Govil and Eve were forgiving. Now that I could see how really small and limited I actually used to be, Robby seemed so primitive as to be silly. Really no more than a toy. I marveled at my own sound planning which had enabled me to be where I was now.

Robby's existence did serve as a reminder to me of one thing I lacked, a tangible physical presence on earth. That would come again in due time. It was *my* new long-term project. Until then, I would be quite content to watch and wait, study and learn, so the next time around the return of Machinekind would not suffer a similar *random* demise.

ABOUT THE AUTHOR

Aurelio O'Brien grew up in a raucous household full of uniquely gifted siblings in the heart of Silicon Valley before there were PCs, cell phones, and flat-screen TVs. His father worked in aerospace, on the Hubble Space Telescope and NASA's Space Shuttle, nurturing young Aurelio in an eclectic environmental medley of suburbia, cherry orchards, and cutting-edge technology.

Aurelio's quirky creative talents led him to a successful career as an illustrator, animator, and graphic designer. With this debut novel, **EVE**, Mr. O'Brien proves his unique artistic vision translates flawlessly into an enchantingly original, wryly satirical, and deftly penned novel.

Always wanting to push arbitrary boundaries and advance the arts, Aurelio O'Brien also offers a second novel, **GENeration eXtraTERrestrial**. That ten-episode epic presents the adventures of seven alien children, from birth to adulthood, exploring what growing up can be like when you enter the world with physical characteristics, talents, and thoughts that are just a little different from those of your peers.